What the critics are saying…

5 Stars! "The writing style is beautiful…it flows well and it is easy to get caught up in this wonderful book that I will read again!" ~ *Anya Khan Just Erotic Romance Reviews*

5 Stars! "…a delicious tale of Robin Hood from a whole new perspective… The love scenes are alive with emotion and flaming hot sexual tension. *Ms. Ladley* has struck gold yet again with her unique ability to create rich, vibrant plots and intricate characters that leave the reader begging for her next offering." ~ *Keely Skillman EcataRomance Reviews*

4 Stars! "Sensually alluring while being a great story, *A Wanton's Thief* is a story that fans of medieval times and paranormal stories will love, I certainly did." ~ *Sheryl eCataRomance reviews*

An Ellora's Cave Romantica Publication

www.ellorascave.com

A Wanton's Thief

ISBN # 1419952978
ALL RIGHTS RESERVED.
A Wanton's Thief Copyright© 2005 Titania Ladley
Edited by: Briana St. James
Cover art by: Syneca

Electronic book Publication: May, 2005
Trade paperback Publication: November, 2005

Excerpt from *Me Tarzan, You Jewel*
Copyright © Titania Landly, 2005

Warning:

Also by Titania Ladley:

A Wanton's Thief

To the Reader:

The tales of the infamous Robin Hood and his Merry Men have been told and re-told in many ways over the centuries. It is thought in some accounts that the bandit, who reportedly stole from the rich to provide for the poor, first emerged during the reign of King Henry II in the twelfth century. Some place him during the later era of King Richard—or Richard the Lionhearted—son of Henry II and Eleanor of Aquitaine, Queen of England and former Queen of France. And yet other stories set him within the thirteenth, fourteenth or fifteenth centuries. Each telling is different, each version of this outlaw legend more exciting than the last. But what of the notations of speculation on wizardry or magic associated with the elusive desperado?

What, indeed?

Thus I bring you my version, that of magic and sorcery, spells and immortal life. Meet my "Robin Hood", a charming rogue of the supernatural, a thief of not only a sixpence or two, but of a young maid's heart and her blazing desire to be set free. And what a better explanation to Robin Hood sightings in various centuries and locales than that of an immortal hero who moves through time, who could quite possibly be among us even today...

Dedication

To Tara, my one and only little girl. This one is for you, a lover of romance and chivalry, magic and passion. I love you, sweet daughter, and even though you're all grown up now, you'll always be my precious baby girl.

Chapter One
Northern England
Early November 1536
Wyngate Hall

"Lady Salena must die."

At the terse, ominous tone, Falcon Montague stiffened within the confines of his hiding place. Standing still between the thick drapes and the cool frosted glass of the veranda door, he narrowed his eyes, attempting to peer through a tiny slit in the fabric. His heart pounded with excitement and curiosity. If the inhabitants of the study knew the infamous "Robin Hood" eavesdropped on them, the hounds of hell would be set loose in a matter of seconds. But not before he could inflict his share of mayhem upon the sorry chaps.

To silently emphasize his point, he flexed his hand around the solid gold candelabra he'd just plucked up before the occupants had entered the library not moments ago. Unable to spy the figures through the minute opening, he perked his ears instead, and listened intently to the murder plot he'd suddenly become privy to.

"But how, sir? She has very loyal staff surrounding her day and night." The voice grew deeper, softer, as if the man leaned in to continue in utmost confidence. "I daresay, however, her chambermaid could be disposed of easily, making way for the task as our lady slept. But still, are you certain…?"

"Am I certain?" the other voice hissed, bringing to mind the devil in his sourest of moods. "Does the sun not rise every morning? Of course I'm certain, you fool! She cannot live here — or anywhere — any longer. There is no other way about it. Wyngate Hall, though her home since birth, will no longer be hers as long as you do as you are told. Do you understand?"

"Yes, sir. I understand completely that she can no longer remain as the mistress of Wyngate Hall and that her dowry will not be leaving this keep...if things go as planned." The man sighed. "But I suppose you wish *me* to do the dubious honor of seeing to her termination?"

Falcon suppressed a jerk when the reverberation of a fist pounding down upon wood sounded in the room.

"No," the tyrannical one sneered. "I wish myself to do it."

"You do?"

The insolent man snorted sarcastically. "You idiot! No. It *must* be by someone other than myself. As a favorite at court, Salena carries with her automatic protection. Henry would have my head upon a platter if he were to discover I'd seen to her demise. If she should turn up dead—and she will—I cannot be blamed. You hear me, man? Do you hear me? You must cover your tracks and you must be careful. I *will* have her fortune, but without suspicion. So it must look like an accident—and *before* she marries the duke, Edward Devonshire, in a fortnight. Before he claims her riches and satisfies his horrific debts with every last shilling of her fat dowry."

"B-but...no matter who performs the dastardly deed itself, the king will most likely uncover all involved, eventually. Therefore," the man said with an audible swallow, "he'll have *my* head on that platter."

Falcon heard wood grate against wood and the undeniable smack of a chair toppling onto the hard floor. "If I do not have your head first."

The other man gasped. "No, please!"

"Please, what?" In his mind, Falcon could almost see the perpetrator's eyebrows rising in mockery.

"I shall perform your bidding with extreme precision. Please, I...I..."

"Very well. Now, it seems we suddenly see eye to eye." Falcon heard the tightness of the smile in the gloating tone. "See to it immediately, cover your tracks well and you will be rewarded handsomely...as soon as she's dead."

"Yes, sir. Right away, sir." The quivering voice moved nearer and Falcon caught a brief glimpse of the backside of a man of average height and build with mousy brown hair. Its texture failed to gleam even by the light of the fat candle burning in the sconce near the door, as if the fellow lacked a sufficient, nutritious diet. He moved quickly to the portal just out of Falcon's sight. "I shall implement a plan this very night. By morning, your command will be...old news. Our lady will be dead."

"Good. Good. Now, be gone with you. I feel a sudden headache coming on and wish to retire."

"I...yes, I will report back to you first thing at sunrise. Good night to you." The sliding study door whooshed open and shut. Once the man had exited, all Falcon could hear for the longest time was the ticking of the clock on the mantel. He closed his eyes, beads of perspiration trickling down his spine despite the chill of the glass at his back. The musky smell of the drapes filled his nostrils and swirled sickeningly in his stomach. He longed to be gone from the stuffy confines of this sudden prison, to snatch up what he'd come for and be on his merry way. But now it seemed there would be another jewel to confiscate.

Lady Salena Tremayne.

Ah, yes, the arrogant, prim and bewitching daughter of the deceased Earl of Herringrose. With the exception of this very night, prior to entering through the library veranda door, Falcon had seen her but once through the slit of his helmet at the king's annual jousting tournament. He'd promptly lost that competition due to disrupted concentration and the annoying bulge in his braies.

A swish of fabric and a clomp of boots on wood sounded across the room, jolting Falcon from the erotic direction of his thoughts. Through the tiny crack in the curtains, it was all he could do to strain and watch as a pair of hands drew out a key from behind a stone above the hearth. The tall figure, nothing but a dark silhouette against the firelight, moved to the left of the fireplace, just out of Falcon's range. He heard the insertion of the key, the click of metal against metal, the slide of a drawer. And the angry crumple of paper.

"The bitch!" the man growled. "You'll die, Salena. You'll die this very night."

Falcon stood stiff and ready as the drawer slammed shut and the snap of the lock echoed, melding with the tune of the crackling fire. Holding his breath, the thud of his heart choking him, Falcon listened as heavy footsteps neared. His hand tightened around the candlestick. Mentally preparing himself, he stood ready to strike at the first sign of discovery. But luck would be with him this night. He sighed when the study door slid open and shut, and the footfalls of a murderer gradually died off into the distance of the great hall.

Cautiously, Falcon pushed aside the drapes. He grimaced when his elbow tapped the window behind him. Waiting, he cocked his head but heard no returning footsteps. Slipping from the half-open gap, he stealthily stepped toward the small side table positioned to the left of the hearth. On his way, he replaced the candelabra on the massive mahogany desk set before the paned French doors. Soaked from his confinement behind the drapes he avoided the heat of the fire, despite the chill in the November air. Reaching for the one drawer hidden within the elm side table, he jiggled the handle. It wouldn't budge. His eyes rose to the area of stones set above the mantel where he'd seen the man remove the rocky protrusion and withdraw the key.

A creak of boards sounded above his head. His gaze shot upward and he sighed, knowing that meant someone was still about, possibly on their way downstairs.

He shook his head. There was no time to search for the paper. He must ascend to the upper level and locate Lady Salena's chamber immediately. Clearly, he'd have to be patient. It would be necessary to return in the future to investigate the telling document the man had wadded up in anger and stored in the locked drawer. Hopefully, it would still be there and would provide the clue Falcon needed to confirm his growing suspicions.

Clenching his jaw with regret and irritation, he spun on his leather boots and crept to the door. Sliding one panel open just enough to poke his head through, he furtively regarded the long candlelit corridor of the richly furnished manor. Woven tapestries, gold-framed self-portraits and high-backed, heavy walnut settees lined the arched passageway. Deafening, eerie silence filled his ears. The pungent odor of beeswax and tallow drifted down from the heavy wood and iron candle beam supports dangling above. A sweeping wood staircase descended along the wall to his right. But he'd be a fool to climb it, he mused, swiftly assessing his plan of action. Servants could be about, or the gentlemen from the study could return at any moment.

Instead, Falcon darted left and hugged the cold, stone wall. He shot in and out of alcoves and recessed porticos until he reached the darkened rear of the hall. And there, just as he'd suspected, rose the narrow servants' stairwell. He first tested one step, leaning his weight upon its expanse. Pleased that it made not so much as a minor squeak, he took them two at a time and followed the curved, steep path. Emerging on an upper landing, he noted the absence of light below the portal he hoped would lead to the upstairs bedroom chambers. Slowly, he pushed open the door, relieved that it was indeed the long hallway of suites he sought.

It had been on his approach to the stone castle not an hour before that he'd gotten that brief second glimpse of Salena as she'd drawn near her upstairs chamber window and pulled the shutters in against the chilly night air. He'd stood there beneath the gnarling, leafless oak gazing up at her, utterly transfixed by her beauty. She'd paused, staring out pensively into the moonless black of night, the firelight from within shimmering upon her hair. It had immediately brought to mind a long curtain of rich, sable fur, the glory of it silhouetting her in a sexual, fire-edged glow. And, like a lovesick, foolish lad, he'd indulged himself in the fantasy of running his fingers through its silky, soft tresses while sinking himself between her legs.

"Enough, Falcon," he whispered to himself.

Mentally, he ascertained which chamber door would be hers based on the position of the window he'd seen her in. And he darted to it, noting with disappointment that light filtered below the closed door. So, he wouldn't have the luck of an easy abduction after all, for it seemed the maiden remained awake.

Getting right to the chore, he turned the ornate crystal door handle and slipped into the antechamber of her suite. The chambermaid's rumpled straw pallet within the alcove was vacant, just as he suspected it might be. Apparently, the murder plot had already begun with the calling away of Lady Salena's personal servant. Would they have attempted to win over the servant and include her in the plot? Perhaps poisoning of Salena's food by the maid or smothering her in her sleep? Or would the villains eliminate the maid altogether, later enter the lady's chamber, do the deed directly or possibly see that she suffered a deadly riding accident on the morrow? Well, there wasn't time to determine the exact plan, but Falcon knew he must immediately remove her from any impending danger.

Yet that wasn't the reason his heart pounded and fluttered in anticipation.

No. He had nothing to fear from Lady Salena's death or the men who planned it, for he would alter fate this very moment and see that she lived. Neither did he worry over the necessary, lifesaving deed of kidnapping he was about to implement.

What Falcon Montague feared was his fiercely guarded heart suddenly coming under siege again.

And when he caught sight of her lying in sensual slumber upon the massive bed, the warm glow of fire dancing upon her ethereal beauty, he could have sworn an arrow pierced his heart and brought him to his very knees.

* * * * *

16

Even from the depths of sleep, Salena sensed she wasn't alone. Clawing her way to awareness, she slowly opened her eyes. Her heart galloped in her chest as she stared up at the hangings of gold-fringed, royal blue velvet draped from the bedstead. Studying one tassel in order to keep herself grounded, she inhaled and caught the wild scent of forest and…man?

She gasped and sat upright. Having fallen asleep in a diagonal position across the bed, she suddenly became aware of the narrow space between the side of the bed and the wall behind her. Aware, lord help her, of the fact that she sensed that very space was no longer empty.

A large, hot hand clamped over her mouth before she could tell her limbs to move. An arm, thick and strong, hooked around her and held her own arms captive at her sides. That musky scent of man intensified, and with it, the heat of a beast blanketed her backside.

"Shh. Don't scream. Don't utter a word." The voice, a deep timbre edged with danger, filled her left ear and coiled down long and slow into her abdomen. Salena stiffened against the wall of a rippled, steely chest. Fear overrode the pleasant sensation of warmth, and she wiggled and thrashed, releasing a muffled, feral screech.

"I said don't scream." The arm shook her as he growled out the command. "Do you want to die?"

Her eyes widened. *Of course I don't wish to die!*

"Then shush."

Terror gripped her to the marrow of her bones. Trembling, she shook her head violently, fighting against the shame of tears. Through the blur of them, she searched her chamber for a possible weapon. Her nervous gaze darted across the blue and gold Turkish carpet to the pair of Flanders chairs set before the blazing hearth. Somewhere — was it in one of the chairs or upon the side cupboard? — the small tapestry she'd been embroidering held a large needle. And set upon the low table between the chairs, her late dinner tray remained, a blessed knife still stabbed into the thick hunk of bread remaining there.

Panting, her eyes suddenly shifted to the chest set against the footboard of her bed.

She had a dagger inside! Hope flourished behind her breastbone. Maybe if she could distract the intruder, or play dead or...

With quick decisiveness, Salena relaxed and ceased her thrashing, feigning a swoon. The interloper sighed and loosened his grip. Waiting for the perfect moment to escape, she shivered inwardly when one large hand petted her hair. Salena could swear she heard the erratic thud of the man's heart, as well as that of her own. Shimmers of something altogether strange and yet pleasant rippled through her blood and settled between her legs. Shocked at her body's traitorous reaction, Salena focused instead on the crackle of the fire, the shift of a burning log, the sound of the autumn night wind howling about the outer walls of the keep. She forced herself to ignore the woodsy aroma and heat of the man now holding her tenderly in his arms.

And with quick, nimble precision, she darted from the circle of his arms and scrambled from the bed.

She was across the room with the knife in her hand in a flash. The bulk of her nightrail spun around with her in a flurry of silk and lace. She faced the intruder headlong, her gaze riveting to him where he remained kneeling on the opposite side of her bed.

"Don't you come near me!" Above the glint of the fire off the sterling silver blade, she got her first full perusal of him. Wide and thick of shoulder, his frame seemed to dwarf her massive bed. As she studied him, he came off the mattress and stood to his full height. Her eyes widened. *The man was a bloody giant!*

"Hello, Lady Salena. How are you this lovely autumn eve?"

With that deep English woodsman's dialect that seemed to caress her ears, he crossed to her, his thick arms folded mockingly over his chest. That scent of wild outdoors filled her nostrils once again and did strange things to her insides. She took in the mannish sway of the Lincoln-green cloak, the tautness of the dark brown, leather jerkin over a wide torso. And beneath the bulky garment, she caught a glimpse of a white linen shirt in stark contrast to the bronzed skin of his neck. Nervously, her gaze sank lower to that narrow pelvis and shocking...*area* of his anatomy. The codpiece he wore over his crotch was attached in the manner of the less fortunate, by leather strappings and cords. His braies, she noted with a hot flush to her cheeks, were snug over finely muscled thighs and calves, and disappeared into shin-high, leather riding buskins.

"H-how do you know my name?"

He lifted one long, bronzed finger to his pursed lips and simply said "Shh..." as he moved nearer.

Those full lips stunned her and she gasped at the erotic turn of her thoughts, the fantasy of her mouth melded with his. In shocking response, hot dampness flooded her inner thighs. But she ignored it, her heart pounding as she forced herself to remain brave, to study the intruder who caged her inside her own chambers like an untamed beast of Sherwood Forest.

She couldn't see his entire face due to the black mask he wore. It covered him from mid-forehead, down over the bridge of the straight nose, across the upper half of his cheeks. Just looking at such a clandestine man made her heart race with some sort of odd excitement blended with trepidation. And to think he stood in her chamber...and she was alone with him!

Forcing her gaze to study him further, she noted the thick length of arrow-straight, white-gold hair streaming from the side confines of the mask's ties. It fell down and behind the beefy shoulders eliciting from her a strange curiosity at what it might be like to comb her hands through the long strands. On his head he wore a feathered woodsman's hat to match the very shade of his cloak. And sticking up behind the broad shoulders and curtain of hair rested the unmistakable jut of a longbow, iron-tipped arrows and the bulk of a worn, bulging gunnysack.

But it was the slits in the mask her gaze kept flitting back to. Through the openings, Salena finally spied the eyes. Her breath caught in her chest. Somehow familiar to her, she furrowed her brow, struggling to place the undeniable deep green, almond-shaped orbs. They sparkled with an almost magical sheen, holding her captive, rendering her spellbound against her will.

"Who…who are you?" Damning her trembling hand, she waved the blade in his face.

He lifted one corner of those thick lips and stared into her eyes with unwavering intent. "You should bloody well know that already, milady." He took one more step until she had to tilt her head back to see through the slashes and into the emerald eyes.

"I swear I'm going to scream if you venture one more step nearer." And to emphasize her bravado, she held the knife up to his neck, the blunt tip pressing into the tanned flesh. She watched, suddenly fearless and empowered, when his pulse leapt next to the blade's edge, dancing in rhythm to the flames in the hearth that shone upon his masked face.

"I'll ask you again, beautiful maiden…" He ignored the weapon and lifted a lock of her hair, rubbing it between his fingers. Salena fought the heaviness of her eyelids, the fire that seemed to scorch her from the surface of her scalp to her womb. Confusion gripped her, for this fire had nothing to do with the one in the hearth so near her side. No, this flame was one altogether different, altogether unfamiliar. Yet maddeningly, it tempted her, made her long to draw closer to the source.

"Do you want to die?"

That oddly pleasant blaze was instantly doused with the coldness of his recurring question. Fear reared up to scorch her with ruthlessness, like that of a fire-breathing, lethal dragon.

"What a ridiculous question." She slapped his hand away and freed her hair from his grip, attempting to emit composure. "I vow with all my strength to fight you," she hissed. "For I wish to live, just as anyone else does." And she raised her chin and narrowed her eyes to further emphasize her conviction.

He chuckled, a reverent song that seeped into the back portal of her soul. Catching her off guard with the laxness of his mood, his hand was suddenly around her wrist, squeezing the very blood from her veins. The knife fell to the carpet, tumbled end over end and clattered against the stones of the hearth.

"And I vow with all my strength to keep you alive." He yanked her into his arms. Salena's breath whooshed from her lungs when he slammed her against the rock-hard wall of his chest. Heat and all-male power engulfed her. The wet spot between her thighs throbbed with a sudden vengeance. Her system pulsed, choking her voice box so that she couldn't so much as squeak out a protest. As he spoke low and soft, his breath fanned her cheek. The tone and rhythm of it reminded her of the pants and gasps of a couple's passionate embrace, like that that she'd spied at a recent ball when she'd happened upon lovers in the gardens.

What ailed her? she wondered, panicked. This intruder clearly threatened her, yet her traitorous mind and body kept twisting everything into dangerous, irresistible lasciviousness, making her think of things she normally kept at bay.

"So you declare to keep me alive yet you stealthily enter my home like a common thief. Next, you awaken me from a deep sleep, threaten me and accost and terrorize me in my own private chambers." She twisted within the circle of his arms, gasping when her nipples abraded over the rough leather of the jerkin he wore. The areolas hardened into painful, aching pebbles, protruding shockingly against the silk and lace of her nightgown's bodice. "If you do so speak the truth, sir, then...*let. Me. Loose!*"

Her fists pounded against that chest in a flurry. But he didn't so much as flinch. He merely tightened his grip on her, thereby omitting the meager space she'd had available for her attack.

"I say, keep quiet, woman! If you value your life, do not make another sound." He growled it out, his wet mouth plastered against her right ear. Lord help her, but a trail of heavy desire plunged from her ear into her breast, and suffused straight down into her mons. Slowly, as if she'd consumed a potent poison, it moved into her legs and left them trembling in weakness. As she panted shamefully like a mutt in heat, his sharp intuition sensed her dilemma and he hauled her up against him so that her feet dangled off the floor.

Which brought her engorged clitoris up firmly against his codpiece...and no doubt the thickness that hid beneath it. It was a sensation she'd only dreamed about before now. Even her own inexperienced, fumbling masturbation late at night in her bed had always been unfulfilling and anti-climactic. Not even her one secret mating encounter with Thane Mathews—rest her former fiancé's caddish soul—two years ago had produced a smidgen of what she felt right now with this stranger.

Oh, and God forbid, if anyone should discover she'd lost her maidenhead before marriage! She'd been a fool to fall for Thane's charms, to fancy herself in love and to allow her curiosity to win out. A wanton need she hadn't been able to name had driven her to such irreversible, unbearable shame. Salena didn't know what she would do on her upcoming wedding night to her newest betrothed, Edward Devonshire. She hadn't the faintest idea how to disguise her physical state of disgrace. Scorn and embarrassment were sure to play a role once her new husband took her to his bed. She could only hope punishment wouldn't be included—or would be mild enough to withstand. But nonetheless, she would have it coming to her. That one encounter with Thane had been a huge, disappointing mess in which she'd sacrificed her virginity for nothing. She'd turned him away after that and had vowed to never let it happen again until after marriage.

The reality of the stark contrast between then with Thane and now with this stranger hit her headlong, and an involuntary whimper escaped from between her parted lips. Time wavered into nothingness; the fire crackled in the quiet of the room. She clutched the rocky bulges of his shoulders and her eyes slowly rose to meet his. The twinkle of two gems stared back at her through the mask. Something about it, about the clandestine, mysterious look of him, made her think of a wily fox on the hunt for his mate. And the thrill of being that hunted she-fox stole through her in one perilous lash of reality.

"In answer to your previous inquiry, the name's Falcon Montague," he whispered hoarsely, his mouth but a breeze's space from hers.

She'd forgotten that she'd even asked the question. "Falcon Montague." Salena whispered it back, astounded, the name sliding over her tongue sensuously. "The poor loser of King Henry's jousting tournament? The knight who paid no mind to his opponent and openly ogled me as I watched from the stands?"

He barely pressed his lips to hers, the softness of them making her eyelids flutter shut and that spot at her juncture ache to be stroked. Against her mouth he rasped, "Loser, aye, due to a most lovely lady of...distraction. Ah, and ogled would only be for starters." His lips dragged back and forth over hers as he spoke, slow and hot, the sweet flavor of cider filling her mouth.

"I made love to you with my eyes," he went on, "through the confines of my helmet's slits. Aye, I had better things to do than protect myself against your brother's incompetent, haphazard lance."

At mention of her brother, something snapped within her. She pushed against him and stumbled back into one of the high-backed chairs set before the hearth. "Nay. You speak falsehoods."

"That I made love to you with my eyes?"

The visions his words conjured up made her flesh warm with mortification and a yearning she had no right entertaining. But she stayed the course, hoping to distract this intruder — who seemed intent on stealing nothing but her breath from her lungs—until her maid Edwina returned from her sudden calling.

"Nay, that my brother Sheldon is not a skilled and careful noble jouster."

"Well," he sniffed, glancing about the suite for what, Salena knew not. "We will have to wait until a later time to debate that argument. Now—"

"We? Later?" She backed away fumbling her way around the seat until she had herself positioned at its backside. Ominous bells reverberated in her head, as if she'd been forced up into the dome of a cathedral. "Sir, I demand that you leave my chamber at once or I shall scream a bloodcurdling cry that will rouse the entire keep. And you, then, will be as good as dead."

He sighed—just simply sighed as if she bored him to utter tears and felt not an inkling of a threat. "Very well. Then you leave me no choice, milady."

So be it, she thought, fully prepared to end this bizarre yet intriguing meeting with the unusual fool intent on his own hanging death. She drew in a lungful of chilly air to ready for the scream. But her voice suddenly became clogged in her throat. Falcon's eyes, those jewels of the very devil, sparked at that precise moment, and the fire in the hearth whooshed upward. Entranced against her will, Salena stared as he neared, slowly rounding the chair until he was at her side. With a hot, firm hand, he turned her so that she was forced to face him squarely and look up into his narrowed gaze. Twin, arrowed beams of green emerged from his liquid eyes enthralling her, completely holding her captive against her will. She could not speak, she could not move, she could not so much as breathe.

"You will not speak. And you will now sit."

No, no! Her mind screamed but her voice would not cooperate. Fear raced through her system, every pulse point in her body pounding hard and loud like that of a musician's drum at court. She swallowed the lump that had lodged in her windpipe and gasped when her legs began to move without her ordering them to do so. With purpose and subservient strides, she brushed past him, ignoring the magical power that seemed to glow about him. Her body obeyed and she sat in the chair, mute. Panic began to churn into something altogether different. Unable to move or speak, she kept her gaze fixed on the dancing inferno within the stone hearth. Anger simmered inside her, rolling to a full boil.

Her unblinking stare moved to him. She watched, helpless as he stalked to a coffer and flipped open the lid. Hurriedly, he yanked his gunnysack from his shoulder, pulled it open and set it on the floor before the chest. Immediately, several familiar items caught her eye when he rummaged through the sack seeming to make room for more bounty. She saw her brother's large medallion amulet, her father's solid gold bookends, their ornate silverware passed down through many generations of Tremaynes and, collectively, worth a pretty pound.

Her face warmed when he tossed and dug through the contents of her personal storage — oh, how she hated this man! He drew out a pair of her riding boots, two of her older gowns she normally wore for gardening and several grooming and toiletry articles. Mortified, she watched as he held up various undergarments, burying his face in the fluff of them before stuffing them into his bag.

What was this man doing? Heavens help her, she was under the complete spell of a madman! She longed to scream, to demand answers to her questions. To flee!

But she had no strength in her legs, no voice, no answers and he offered no explanations. Many more questions jumbled in her brain as he continued his free rein of her suite.

He didn't stop with her personal hidden items. Next, he crossed to the wall and plucked her thickest cape from a hook. Taking long strides, he breezed by the chest and snatched up his sack, then came to stand before her. Kneeling, he shoved her feet into the boots and fastened them. "Stand up."

Again, her body obeyed while her mind shouted in silent protest. He rose and swirled the fur-lined cloak around until it covered her shoulders. Fastening the wrap, those long, adept fingers moved up her collarbone to her neck. Even as gentle heat embraced her and slid down reluctantly into her womb, she could have sworn he was about to choke her. But instead, he raised the hood of the wrap and covered her head. His scent, now warmed by the fire at his back, incensed her, abducting her olfactory nerves in such a way that she longed to pinch her nose against the pleasing aroma of him.

And she wondered with a mixture of amazement and ire how it could be that this man could instill fear in her one moment, and yet shocking desire the next.

It was this dark magic of his. There could be no other explanation. If he didn't possess these tricks of wizardry, he would not be able to possess her in *any* manner whatsoever!

Footsteps fell upon the wooden plank of the outer threshold. Her eyes widened and hope flourished in her chest. *Yes! I'm inside. I'm here. Please, Sheldon, Edwina,* someone *help me!*

He narrowed his eyes as they riveted toward the door. Once again, beams of energy shot from them. The footfalls stopped in the corridor outside her chamber. She heard voices, then an abrupt silencing. And the sounds of help, of her one salvation, retreated into the quiet of the hall.

"Just a bit of gentle persuasion," he said with the flash of a wolfish grin. "Now, we must go."

He quietly settled the fully stuffed gunnysack over his shoulder. His eyes held her spellbound, and he spoke with a deep, almost intimate command. "Turn and cross to the door. Open it. Check for servants, family, anyone. If and only if there is no one about, you will exit into the corridor, turn right, and descend the rear servants' staircase. I will follow immediately behind you. Once we reach the lower level, you will lead me outdoors through the safest rooms and portals. You will only go where there are no other people about. When we reach the outdoors, you will allow me to escort you to my steed. And then together, we will mount and be on our way."

Her teeth ground together in anger. Salena attempted once again to scream, to run, to disobey this obvious sorcerer who held silent powers over her body that she could not control. But it was no use. Though she glared back with eye-power of her own, the magic proved too strong to fight, despite the inner rebelliousness that spewed from her soul.

With tears of frustration brimming in her eyes, Lady Salena Tremayne, betrothed of Duke Edward Devonshire, turned and walked briskly toward the door. Out into the cold of an autumn night, the future Duchess of Oxford stole away with the thief who held all she desired, and all she hated and feared.

Chapter Two

Bareback upon his Friesian warhorse, Falcon held Salena before him, her soft, womanly curves shivering against his jerkin and codpiece. The braies beneath his cloak stretched painfully taut over the erection he'd sported since spying her slumbering form upon that queen's bed of hers. Inhaling, he caught the scent of roses and something altogether feminine, distinct to only this woman. It played havoc on his senses, nearly rendering him unable to perform his required spells of protection. His cock throbbed with the need to claim the pussy that he knew, despite her outward indignation and anger, had filled with honey at his nearness.

But first he had to get her to the safety of his village a day's ride from here.

They reached the gatehouse and Falcon looked up at the lone gatekeeper. He sent his *tazir* gaze into the man's eyes, enthralling him.

"Guard, you will release the drawbridge over the moat, and once we have passed, you will return it to its former state and never recall this exchange."

"Yes, sir," the man called down, his voice in a monotone of obedience.

The clank and grind of iron chains sounded as the sentry lowered the drawbridge. Behind him, Falcon could hear the shouts of panic, the low squall of an alarm as Lady Salena's absence was made known to the loyal members of her keep.

"Hurry, man!"

"It is nearly done," the guard informed him. And indeed it was. Even as the wooden planks crashed to the far stone edge of the moat, Falcon urged his mount to leap upon the bridge and spurred it across the long stretch. The clatter of hooves thundered out, echoing in the moonless dark of night. He heard the creak and clang of metal as the watchman raised the bridge behind him.

Knowing he hadn't the full powers to enthrall and escape an entire army of knights, Falcon urged his steed on, putting as much distance between them and the castle as humanly possible.

As they traveled on and the silver moon began to peep through the waning clouds and crooked trees overhead, Falcon started to relax. Behind him, the wilderness stretched, as did mile after mile of barren land. His trail had been lost. The pursuing soldiers of Lady Salena's home, Wyngate Hall, had long since taken another path in error. She now slumped against him in exhaustion. The power he'd cast on her still remained, so he roused her with a gentle nudge.

"Awaken."

She stirred and her eyes rose to his in that slow manner of one *tazired* by his allures. His breath caught when the hue of them shone up at him, twinkling by the moonlight. They were a warm, almost spooky peacock-blue edged with sleepy bliss. Thick midnight lashes framed the unusual catlike shape of them, fanning her high cheekbones as she blinked. Slowly, awareness dawned in them, and he knew the exact moment that anger stirred within her breast once again. The full cherry lips pursed and he fought a craving to suck them right into his mouth. The pale skin flushed to the pink of a rose. He clenched one hand against the reins, fighting the urge to explore every silky inch of her flesh.

Falcon reminded himself that involvement with a mortal always amounted to nothing but emotional suicide. But his blood rekindled, despite the firsthand experience of the repeated heartaches he'd endured, watching helpless, as each of his mortal lovers throughout the past decades and centuries had died off.

Shaking the morbid thoughts, he allowed the fire to settle to a boil within his balls, and the sac throbbed with a demanding vengeance. Falcon tightened his hold on her, grinding her hip into his penis as he held her gaze, entranced by her witch's charm. Suddenly, he understood how one must feel to be under his own *tazing* spells. And her eyes, coupled with that intoxicating ire, were far more potent than his own.

"You are released from submission—for the moment." He looked away, breaking the tie that held her bound to his dominance.

He needed no powers to tell the exact second she realized she was free. But Falcon was prepared. With one hand, he kept a sure grip on the reins. He clamped his thighs around the stallion to keep them both safely mounted. His arms closed around her upper body, pinning her elbows to her sides.

And she thrashed and screeched, bucking against his tight hold.

"You monster!" She tried to hunch her head down to bite his forearm, but he shook her hard enough to prevent the defensive move. "Oh! You'll pay for this. The king and my brother will hunt you down. You will die, Falcon Montague. You will die a choking death at the gallows—and hopefully suffer some rotting in prison before you should be so lucky."

"Madam, you do so break my heart with your penchant for vengeance."

She twisted then, and shot him a loathing look. "*Vengeance? That is but a smidgen of what I wish upon you. You have entered my home uninvited, apparently stolen from my family's coffers—*" she glowered at the bulge of loot upon his back, "*—accosted me in my own private chambers and abducted me from the safety of the only home I have ever known.*"

He grinned down at her. "You've forgotten the fact that I've set out to deflower you for your betrothal to the very stodgy but still alive Duke of Oxford."

"He is not stodgy!" she shrieked.

Falcon guided the horse up a sharp incline and turned deeper into the woods. "I beg to differ." And to prove his point, he dragged her hip back and forth over his erection. "Do you feel that?"

Delight stirred within him when she let out an involuntary whimper of mortification—or was it desire? "How could I not? It stands erect like a bloody lance between us!"

He threw his head back and roared. "Aye, good point. But do you see *my* point?"

When she remained mute, her jaw clamped, and presented him with her regal profile, he went on. "The duke is beginning to gray, his skin is showing signs of shriveling and it is said that his…lance…is no longer in working order."

"You lie!"

"I tell naught but truths, young, beautiful maiden. And to add further fact to my 'tales', he's also—reportedly, of course—in dire need of a very rich dowry to pull his estate out of the deep bowels of his gambling sickness. And it is my understanding that you, milady, possess a sizable dowry."

She swiped her hood from her head, and he watched as the moonlight speared down upon the long sable locks. Faint auburn highlights glimmered upon the lunar-bathed tendrils. Clouds dissipated in the night sky above, making way for the pinpoint twinkles of stars. Unable to resist, he reached up and combed his hand through the silky curtain until he gripped her nape.

"You are a vile serpent." She slapped at his arm, barely jarring it. "And you get your filthy hands off me this instant!"

"Ah," he rasped, drawing her closer. "But serpents do not have hot, talented hands. They are, however, snakes," he amended, jerking back on the reins until his mount halted, "like that which you've awakened within my britches."

At his words, she went into a flurry of twists and bucks, obviously understanding his esoteric meaning. She growled reminding him of a wild cat fighting to be released from his hold.

"Stop. Stop now or we both will be unseated."

She let out an unladylike snort. "Oh, how I pray to God that you end up on the earth with a smarting backside—and a broken neck besides!"

Well, there was no other way about it. Falcon did not wish either of them to break their necks. He gripped her face and turned her so that she was forced to look into his eyes.

"You will stop this foolishness immediately!"

His powers hit her as a stone might fly from a catapult and strike a castle wall. She instantly jolted and stilled her movements, slumping against him.

"And now that you've stirred my manhood, something must be done to…relieve me. But not until you're ready of your own free will."

He tipped her chin up and watched, once again enchanted when defiance sparked in her eyes. "You may talk to me only, but you may not scream or alert anyone else we may encounter. You may only move your body if you're in need of a change of position for the sake of comfort…or if you genuinely wish to seek out my…charms."

"I…I…your *manhood* will not be relieved by me."

"That is your choice."

"I have no choices in this matter!"

Unable to resist, he massaged her bottom lip with the pad of his thumb. Her eyes went limpid with what could only be desire. "No, you don't have a choice in whether you remain at Wyngate Hall or not. But…"

"But?"

"But you do have a choice as to whether or not I kiss you. And, oh, I do wish to do just that." Her eyes widened and sparkled in the moonlight. They made him think of the many precious gems he'd stolen over the centuries. Only the worth in the cut of them, the passionate gleam she could not hide from him, made them far more valuable than any loot he'd seized before. He watched as her chest rose and fell, listened to her uneven, wispy breathing. Clearly, she warred with her own scruples, but he would not force the issue even if she chose to deny what was apparent in every aspect of her being.

"A kiss?"

He nodded, his heart captured by her astonished and curious tone. "A kiss. Just grant me one chance to sample your flavor. One chance and I promise, if you do not like it, I will never plea for your charms again."

She lifted her chin. "That is quite a noble vow for such a criminal man."

"Criminal or not, it is by my honor I swear it."

"And you promise you will never force me against my will by use of your bizarre, paralyzing and mind-controlling black magic?"

"I promise to never force my amorous needs upon you, Lady Salena. You must be willing, for I prefer my women eager for my advances. I will only use those powers on you when necessary to preserve your safety, but not in the case of courting…and all that goes with it."

She let out a melodious, cynical tinkle of laughter. "Courting? Is that what you're doing, courting me after an abduction?"

Her cheek felt satiny against his palm, a maddening stimuli when one had a painful erection to rival a mountain. "It hadn't been part of my original plan just as the abduction hadn't, but yes, I desire to woo you into my bed."

She gasped.

"You're rather indignant," he chuckled, "when I happen to know that wet spot between your legs throbs, your heart pounds in anticipation of the coming kiss and your lips tingle with the need to be devoured by mine."

Salena swallowed audibly. "You…how do you know this?"

He trailed a finger down her neck watching with undisguised lust as her eyelids quivered. She let out a strangled groan when he said, "Because I can smell your arousal and because my extensive experience has taught me the look and body language and sounds of a woman who wishes to be taken by a man."

"Taken?"

Falcon sighed sensing her surrender. "We can start with a kiss. Can't we?"

A long moment went by in which she stared into his eyes. The lunar glow waned and ebbed as clouds glided across the night sky. He drew her sweet scent into his lungs unsure as to how much longer he could take this torture of being so very near to her without being allowed to sample her. Finally, she nodded and whispered, "Aye, we can start with a kiss."

And she tipped her head back and parted her lips in fascinated welcome.

* * * * *

With the moon behind him, it seemed he descended upon her like a hungry raven in the night. He still wore that ominous, mysterious black mask, and she thought of a devil seducing her into his lair of dark magic. Hot hands held her face captive while his body seemed to scorch her through the fabric of her cloak and gown. She no longer felt the chill of the midnight hour; in its place simmered something altogether elemental. His magnetic eyes snared her through the mask's slits, intent as a wolf about to tear into his prey. Though his powers once again held her obedient, it was only against any attempts at escape. He did not force upon her his ardent allure but rather dangled it in front of her for the taking. She shivered with anticipation, despite the fury that ate away at her soul at her own self-betrayal.

She caught a whiff of his rugged scent mixed with cool wind just before his lips slammed into hers. Something about it made her hungry, made her yearn for a long drought of him, if only to satisfy her curiosity. The feel of his lips on hers made her suddenly unsure of herself and what propriety and her morals would dictate. This kiss…it was nothing like Thane's kisses had been. Wet and warm, Falcon tasted of a sweet ambrosia that instilled further thirst within her breast. The need caused her to tip her head back, to finally accept his probing tongue into her mouth. With a groan that sounded as if it came from somewhere afar, she hesitantly touched her tongue to his. It seemed the contact sent a jolt of energy from his soul into hers. Liquid heat melted over her heart and pooled into her cunt. As if to reinforce the sensation, to inform her he experienced the same wonder as she, he sighed into her mouth.

His hand slid into her cloak and cupped one breast. It was the first time any man had ever touched her there. Thane's hurried lovemaking had apparently skipped this wondrous step. The incredulity of it shocked her into an erotic fog she could not awaken from. Through the silk of her nightshift, he strummed her nipple. It hardened, and with it, so did the little knot between her labia. She tightened her thigh muscles, attempting to hold in the gush of warm liquid that trickled out of her pussy. But it was no use. A flashflood washed over her, and suddenly, she craved his hand down there at the spot that seemed to need soothing.

*Oh, even though I hate you with a passion, please…*please *touch me…down there.*

He chuckled a low, crazed laugh. The hand that had been at her breast now moved down over her quivering abdomen, down lower still to—oh, Lord God above, help her! That was when she realized his powers were not limited to mental control. They also encompassed reading of the mind.

"Ah, you're a passionate one, love. I knew you wanted it," he said huskily, his teeth nipping at her earlobe at the precise second his finger located her clitoris through the cloth of her nightrail. It nearly unseated her from her sidesaddle position across his lap, despite the hold his powers had over her movements. A bolt of lightning-like impact struck her between her legs, forcing her to yearn for more, for further torture.

But his pretentious words jolted her back into her indignant state of mentality as she struggled to save face against her own shocking surrender to this thieving warlock.

You bastard! You arrogant, pompous thief!

He shrugged. "Debatable point. But this…" he whispered, running that hot hand down her thigh, over her knee to the hem of her gown, "is a sure thing."

She stiffened against the ascent of his palm, the callused texture of it now dragging the gown up and abrading over the flesh of her inner thigh. Sweet Mother Mary, but it made her gasp, made her hips tilt up and forward toward his hand.

"You want it, don't you?"

How could she even coherently piece together an answer to the question he asked when his hand articulated its own distracting language?

"Salena, again, it's your choice, but you must answer me *now*. No…or yes?" It came out gruff and insistent as if he held onto rigid restraint. His anxious demand came followed by a shiver of wanton fire centered in her passage. She was ashamed to realize she'd become clay in his hands. Something about him giving her the power of choice coupled with his almost chivalrous attempts at self-control endeared her heart a small measure to her captor. But she didn't care to admit to such a ridiculous emotional defeat at the moment. She just wanted to focus on how good he was making her feel.

"Yes, yes," she whimpered when the flames of his fingertips swirled higher and brushed her clitoris. And in spite of the power his spell had over her voice and her ability to cry out to others, she let out a torturous growl that echoed throughout the forest when his finger sank through her curls. "Oh, yes, please touch me!"

"Look at me."

The sharp command did little to lesson the magic of his touch. Fire shot through her abdomen when he swirled his finger over the large pebble. Still, she obeyed under the spell's force, turning her head to look into those liquid eyes.

"I want to hear your voice when I bring you pleasure." He said it with a strained tone, and with his words, he ground her hip into the hardened mass within his braies, a mass that now pressed enormous and threateningly against her. Even so, it somehow had the ability to make her long for its length to be within her wet passage. In her limited experience, mating had been painful and disappointing. She'd not felt that actual...supposed bliss before, but had heard whisperings of it from select maids at court. And suddenly, she'd never been so aware of the need to satisfy that particular curiosity and to know what those other women seemed to live for.

"Remember, you may not scream or bring attention in any way to us if we should encounter intruders."

"You are the intruder," she accused on a moan as he slowly and deliberately sank another long finger into her tightness, again something Thane had omitted from the act. Her eyelids fluttered and her vision blurred. She could barely see his masked face beneath the shadow of the woodsman's cap. But she could clearly smell the scent of him mixed with that of her own arousal and the aroma of the horse that stood obediently still beneath them. And like a fire-tipped arrow, his fingers ignited within her, making her arch against her will and against the power of his spell, right into the source of throbbing heat.

"Again, a comment that warrants further consideration. Ah," he said with a strained tone, his breath coming in sharp staccato spurts. "You're so tight...but not still a virgin, I see."

She could have sworn she saw the red, embarrassed glow of her face reflect upon his mask. "Don't say such things, don't talk. Please...I—"

With his fingers still inside her, he hoisted her up. Dragging her against the solid wall of his chest, he positioned her so that she faced forward, her back pressed into his chest. She no longer sat in sidesaddle fashion but astride the horse with one leg dangling on each side. As a proper lady, never before had she sat a horse in this manner. But she had to admit the chilly air was a godsend upon the burning flesh of her legs and pussy. Still unable to move her limbs voluntarily, something feral reared up inside her at the spread position with the warm solid girth of animal held between her legs. Falcon ground her rear against his erect shaft, and Salena thought she'd never experienced a more confusing thing in her life. While her mind screamed harlot, fighting the enthrall of his charms, her body shouted yes, driving toward its own end. It would not obey her commands to resist, to merely move and wrestle for her freedom as a proper woman should do. Nor would it stop with the incessant flood of desire. It was as if she were some court jester's puppet on a string.

And this lack of control infuriated her, made her hate him all the more.

"Talk to me." His hot breath filled her ear, sending shivers down her spine. "Tell me how it feels, how I make you feel."

"I hate you," she said on a gasp as he continued his torture upon her womanhood.

He merely chuckled and dug his heels into the steed's sides. The horse pranced and darted forward upon the path ahead. The jarring sensation of the brisk trot caused his fingers to jolt in and out of her. He swirled the reins around his free hand and found her clit with a leather-wrapped finger.

"Oh, God help me!" Her head fell back against his shoulder. She gulped for air. White clouds puffed from her pursed lips as she panted.

No, it hadn't felt like this before.

He snarled in her ear, his hot mouth buried in her hair, and sucked on the tender flesh of her nape. "He can't help you, Salena. You can only help yourself. Let yourself over to the magic of it, my little dove."

Falcon emphasized that magic by switching to his thumb and increasing the pressure and rhythm. The digit inside her pumped slow and sure, giving her flashes of that never-before-seen pinnacle ahead in the forest of her clogged mind. The hard length of his fingers slid in and out over wet, tight folds, sticky inner recesses. With each penetration, each waggle of his finger more hot juices flowed from inside her, trickling out into his hand, down onto the hide of the horse. She couldn't breathe, couldn't think, could do little else but surrender to this madness.

"Talk to me, milady. How does it feel?"

"It feels..." she gasped, "like sweet sin." Salena couldn't suppress the audible moan that echoed out across the quiet night forest. "I-I can almost taste the delicious desire of it!"

"I heard your thoughts. It's never felt quite like this before, has it?"

"N-no, never."

"Do you like it when I do this?" He flickered his thumb faster, further engorging her knot.

She arched toward his hand. "Yes...oh, yes, I... I *love* it when you do that! Oh," she swallowed, longing to raise her hands up to hold onto him. "Please don't stop. It—something's about to happen, to...to... Oh, heavens, please do it harder, quicker."

He immediately obeyed, and the empowerment of that little bit of control soothed her buried ire one small measure. But she didn't have time to think of that or anything else—not even of the spatters of cold rain that began to fall and sizzle upon her flesh. He tightened his hold on her and lifted her several inches so that his cock was positioned between the mounds of her ass. Pulling her back tighter, the globes—still covered by the fabric of her gown and cape—were forced apart by the thickness of his rod. He twisted and ground her against him, further spreading her ass until she could feel the shaft against her cloth-covered hole. The combined pleasure and shock of it seemed to slap her full-force across the face. She blinked, stiffening automatically at the extremity of such a personal position.

But she couldn't protest for long. On a devil's mission, Falcon whirled her in a dance of utter shame and delicious desire. He ground her hole against the length of him, awakening nerves she didn't know existed. As if that weren't enough, he picked up the cadence of those adept fingers, strumming her with one hand. The other rose to clutch at her breast, plucking the already hard nipple until bolts of pleasure shot down to meet with the inferno at her juncture. The horse trotted on, further jarring her against Falcon's assault.

Breathless, she could no longer restrain herself. "Please, let me raise my arms to hold on to you," she begged, now beyond humiliation, in desperate need of complete fulfillment. With every ounce of strength she possessed, she turned her head so that she could look into his eyes, so that he could transmit to her what she needed. They were but narrowed gems set within the slits of the mask, and she knew then, empowered further by the knowledge of it, that he too felt the loss of control, the euphoric edges of bliss.

"Permission granted. Raise your arms up and behind you, Salena. Hold onto my neck because you're going to need the support when ecstasy claims you."

With a sigh of relief, the tingly sensation in her arms accompanied that of the spell releasing them from its paralyzing hold. Overjoyed by the freedom of it, she shot her arms up behind her and clasped her hands behind his neck. That was all she needed. Now able to gain leverage and press her ass tighter into him, her hole began to twitch and tingle. She could hear the rasping of his breath, feel the hotness of it on her cheek, smell her own juices wafting up to mingle with that of his manly scent. Combined with the cool raindrops falling on her exposed legs, the aura of the mysterious and dark forest that surrounded them, and the fact that he pleasured her as they rode, nothing could have brought her to deeper depths of that unfamiliar bliss.

Except the daggers of hot passion that suddenly — blessedly — pierced her core. The sharp waves of it rippled through her deep center, into her rear, and out over every cell of her body.

"Holy knights of war!" she screamed on a shudder. "Oh, yes! Ah!" she added when one last swell washed through her.

Before she could shake her head and bring herself back to the mortifying reality of what had just occurred, he had her turned upon his lap, once again sitting sideways.

His hand raked through her hair until he held her behind the neck, forcing her to look into his glazed eyes. Salena could smell her own scent upon his hand. She watched, enchanted against her will as the rain dribbled from the brim of his hat and fell cold and spent onto the leather of his jerkin.

He panted, condensation swirling from his mouth and nostrils. "Woman, you tempt me beyond madness. If it weren't for the fact that we must move on quickly, else risk discovery, I'd throw you to the wet earth and sink myself between your beautiful, creamy legs!"

The words had the very same effect on her as his fingers had. But she knew now was the perfect time to use what he'd given her back—free use of her limbs. Jerking her stare from his magnetic one, she made a sudden, rash decision, flung herself from the horse and tumbled to the ground. She heard him curse a profanity at the exact moment her breath was knocked from her.

Salena gasped for air, her chest on fire. *Fool! The bloody horse had to be at least seventeen hands high. And you just barely escaped suicide by daring to jump from the beast's back!*

And too late she realized he still had her legs under siege of his immobilizing spell in which she could only walk if he gave her permission. She could not get up and run! Fear now returning to grip her with the force of a mighty storm, she planted her hands on the soggy, fallen leaves. Salena dragged her inert lower body behind her and into the deep brush with frantic movements. She pulled herself, grimacing at the deadweight her upper body was forced to haul, while her shoulders and arms burned with the effort.

It was then, just when she thought she'd outwitted her captor that her head bumped into a solid trunk. The aroma of

41

wet leather and soil filled her nostrils. Her eyes rounded with fear while her gaze slowly rose up the long length of a pair of legs clad in Lincoln-green braies and knee-high leather boots.

And her heart ceased beating in her chest. Her breath stilled and lodged somewhere inside her windpipe at the picture he made standing there in the drizzly night rain. This fearsome warrior couldn't be the same as the tender man of moments ago who'd given her choices. But she had a feeling her days of options and controlling her own destiny were over.

His fists were planted on narrow hips as he looked down at her. Salena thought she'd never seen a more foreboding sight than that of her ruthless abductor, Falcon Montague, silhouetted against blackened gnarly branches and the fat silver ball of the moon. She couldn't see his eyes through the mask or the shadows, but she knew they were there, felt them touch on her with scorching accuracy.

"Just where do you think you're going?"

She choked on her words. Through gritted teeth, she replied, "Away from you, you—you ogre!"

He clamped his lower lip between his teeth in a lame attempt to stifle the explosive rumble of an amused laugh. "Ogre? You think an ogre could elicit even a smidgen of the passion I easily wrought from you not moments ago, Lady Salena?"

Oh, how she loathed the sound of her name upon his tongue, and yet…

"What do you want from me?" she hissed, digging her fingers into the wet dirt.

"Why, nothing but your safety. You see, I don't wish you to break your bloody neck, my love." He crossed his arms over his chest, the cloak billowing in the chilly breeze. With the mask and the arrogant stance, she thought of a knight at court guarding the king with one eye, while the other roved to plan his next victim of seduction.

"Don't call me that."

"What? My love?"

"Yes, your love. I'm not that in the least, and *never* will be!"

She caught the glint of straight white teeth by a stray beam of moonlight. "We shall see."

"I'll ask you again," she snarled. "What do you want from me?"

"And I'll tell you again, siren." He squatted down on his haunches and pushed back a stray lock of her damp hair. Tenderly, he tucked it behind her ear. Her heart skipped a beat, but she tore her gaze from his before he could enthrall her with his magic. "I seek naught but your safety and preservation of life," he went on.

Damn her traitorous nerves, but the affectionate move nearly rendered her speechless. Nearly. "What, sir, are you babbling about?"

He reached for her, and though she stiffened, she had no choice but to allow him to draw her into his arms. Never mind the fact that she suddenly wanted to be there again. She was no fool. The ground was entirely too cold, wet and uncomfortable to remain as she was. Already, she shivered uncontrollably, though she suspected it was more due to this man than the dank weather.

He rose, her body tucked against his warm chest, and said matter-of-factly, "I *babble* about your life, madam. This very night, I was privy to a conversation within the walls of your own keep that left me no other choice but to rescue you from the sure demise of your impending death."

"Death?" She croaked it out, that word being the last she'd hoped to hear.

He sauntered toward the stallion, glowing eerie and black as coal against the backdrop of dense woods. "Aye, death. I overheard your murder being plotted." He helped her up to the bare back of the beast. The animal snorted in protest, throwing his head back so that she caught her first glimpse of a bright white star on its nose. At Falcon's sharp reprimand, the Friesian calmed obediently. Falcon climbed up behind her, settled in by setting her before him once again and urged the horse onward.

She couldn't help but laugh. "My murder? Sir, you are quite daft. There is no one within my hall who would see me dead. I am loved to distraction by serf, servant and family alike. You must be sorely mistaken — or rather, lying."

He clicked his tongue and the war stallion burst into a gallop. Cold wind rushed up her skirts and blew her hair back against Falcon's chest. "Nay. No mistake." He reached up and placed the hood of her cloak over her head. The move struck another soft spot in her heart, but she forced herself to ignore it.

"True, you're loved by all — all but one man. 'Lady Salena must die' were his exact words. I heard them clear and concise as I hid in the study."

"And why were you hiding? Because you were caught in your act of thievery?"

Salena just didn't — nay, couldn't or wouldn't — believe this man's ridiculous tale. It just wasn't feasible. Everyone loved her — she didn't have a single enemy in all of England, in all of the world! Which led her to believe Mr. Montague plotted something very sinister. Why else would he conjure up such a horrid fable? To make her believe he hadn't really kidnapped her, but in reality, had saved her life? Or perhaps it was to justify in his own sick mind, the illegal activities he'd performed, or to draw attention away from them.

But one question stayed uppermost in her mind…why would a complete stranger not of her castle's territorial realm care if she lived or died? He couldn't possibly be concerned with her well-being — could he?

Ha! She'd be a fool to fall into this diabolical trap of his. Already, he had her spun inside some web of seduction she had difficulty fighting her way out of. But that was only when he used his sorcery upon her — wasn't it? No, she scolded herself. He gave you choices, he allowed you to say no. But she'd said yes. Lord help her, she'd taken leave of all her senses!

Salena settled into the folds of his warm cloak to plan her next attempt at escape and to ponder her most recent behavior. So, to summarize, she thought with self-disgust...she was a woman with hidden, wanton desires in the dangerous company of a lunatic, thieving warlock with deadly hands of magic!

He hefted his gunnysack up to aright its bulk upon his back. "Thief or vigilante. Take your pick, darling."

Unable to help herself, she snorted. "Vigilante? How so?"

"Ah, how is it that I neglected to tell you...?"

The cryptic tone had her twisting about to look up into the shadows of his face. "Tell me what, bandit?"

"That you ride with the infamous outlaw." He tipped his hat in gentlemanly fashion, and she caught the mocking wink as one eye glittered for the briefest moment in the moonlight.

"And who, pray tell, might that be?" she scoffed.

"Why, Robin Hood, of course."

Chapter Three

What was he to do with her now? Falcon asked himself as he looked down into her horror-stricken face. He hadn't thought that far ahead, had only been concerned with her protection, with saving her from the deadly demise those men had been plotting. He'd been a bloody fool to react without thinking ahead.

It suddenly struck him as quite peculiar how his *tazir* abilities had only been used strictly on his enemies until now. He'd never once had to force any woman into submission. Each and every one of them over the centuries—even feisty Maid Marion, rest her soul—had believed in his sincerity and obeyed him when he demanded his lover act in order to preserve her safety and life. Oh yes, it left his braies in a wad just having to admit that Lady Salena didn't trust him. Nor did she believe that he acted in her best interest.

But then again, he'd never before had to abduct a woman from her chambers in the middle of the night. Still, it touched a chord of ire within him that she'd attempted to escape him. They'd been nothing more than mere court acquaintances until this night, true, but did she really think him such an ogre that he'd snatch her from behind the strong walls of her keep just to have his way with her?

He ground his teeth together, wincing as the motion of the horse caused her softness to abrade over his painful erection. But God help him, seeing her abandon and desire as he held her within his embrace had proven to be worth having to deal with her cynical mistrust of him. It was odd, but at the very same time her distrust rankled him, just knowing she despised him outside of the circle of his arms sent him to a whole new level of erotic pleasure he'd not seen before now! It meant his seductive skills as a man were more irresistible to a lady—most importantly, to *this* lady—than he'd even fathomed before now.

"Robin Hood?" Her voice came out on a high-pitched note of revulsion.

With a strange disappointment, he saw the flash of fear and hate in her eyes. But then, that was a common reaction to knowing one was in his infamous company against their will.

"Aye, Robin Hood. Outlaw, thief, supposed murderer." He removed his hat and swirled it, bowing his head sardonically as he held her before him on the horse. "At your humble service."

"You will rot in hell, you brigand! You will be thrown in prison for stealing from my noble and *law-abiding* family—who happens to be under the protection of the king. And you will most definitely hang for abducting a lady of the court!"

Falcon plopped his hat back onto his head. The rain began to spatter down upon them. It suddenly fell in a downpour of icy, fat droplets. She shivered and curled closer into his cloak, despite her obvious aversion to him. Apparently, the lady was no idiot. She'd use and abuse him to her own end, just like all spoiled princesses of her kind. Ah, but she felt warm and womanly against him! And she fit into the curve of his lap as if she'd been made by the heavens specifically for him. Her floral scent rose to tickle his senses, the unique aroma now wetted and stirred anew. He must get her to shelter, get her dry and warm…and he must get himself some sexual relief very soon.

"Ah, well, we shall see. But first things first, milady." And he dug his heels in, spurring the horse onward toward the inn he knew to be just around the next bend.

And toward a certain buxom innkeeper to warm his bones and give him just what he required. That much-needed sexual release.

Lightning flickered in the distance and he heard the rumble of thunder move in. "Warrior, giddy-up!" The stallion burst into action, racing against the wind and rain. Familiar with the destination, he galloped through the intensifying storm, tossing up clods of mud in his wake.

"Hold tight. You shall be snug and dry shortly," he said to her above the clatter of thunder. She stiffened when lightning crashed, striking a nearby tree. The crack of wood followed, along with the whoosh of its falling weight and the acrid scent of smoking wood. But Falcon was a skilled horseman. He maneuvered the steed on, dashing to the side to avoid the falling trunk. It crashed to the forest floor just out of reach of Warrior's hind end.

"Let's go!" The horse obeyed with a neigh, bolting and making an immediate sharp turn off the path.

The inn appeared to be busy this eve, Falcon noted as he passed by the front and rounded one side of the square, two-story, wooden structure. Soft, orange lighting glowed warm and welcoming through the frilly curtains abovestairs. Below, the saloon bustled with the activities of free-flowing spirits and rowdy fun. The sounds of laughter and drunken disagreements drifted out to mingle intermittently with the violent storm. But the inn's apparent abundance of patrons would not stop him from acquiring shelter, this he knew. The innkeeper Molly Pierce never failed to accommodate his every need.

He guided his mount to the stables and let out a low, two-note whistle. Within seconds, a young lad emerged from the dark interior of the structure.

"Mister…Falcon? Is that you?" The boy struggled to keep his voice down, even as the storm seemed to swallow his every word.

Falcon urged Warrior toward the lad. "Aye, Lance. Let Miss Molly know that I am here and in need of shelter for the remainder of the night. And discreetly, as usual, you hear?"

He nodded vigorously. "Who's that you got there, sir?"

"Ah, be gone with you! 'Tis none of your bloody business." He couldn't help but add a chuckle. "Now, remember as always,

I've a pretty coin for you if you do as you're told and keep all your eyes and ears to yourself. And this time, it's a gold one."

Lance leapt up and down in the pouring rain, reminding Falcon of a baby buck pawing to bolt. He barely suppressed a squeal. "Truly, Falcon? Do you truly mean it? A *gold* coin?"

"Aye, and one for your hard-working mother, as well, lad. You go and use the coins wisely with your sweet ma in mind. But first, you must do as I ask you…"

"Right, right! I'm going." He tore out toward the rear entrance to the tavern but suddenly stopped and whirled around. "Falcon?"

"Yes, Lance."

"Thank you. You are a good man, not bad like they say you are."

Falcon nodded. "Go, lad. Go and fetch your mistress."

"Ha! You must have the child brainwashed," Salena scoffed as he dismounted, pulling her with him. She shivered, her small body vibrating against his tightened muscles.

"Nay, not brainwashed. Lance is a smart young man and very dependable." And he shot her a confident grin as he lifted her into his arms and carried her toward the stable's dark interior.

She gazed up into his eyes, rain spattering her lovely heart-shaped face. In that moment, Falcon could swear she *tazired* him by the glittery droplets that clung to the soot-colored lashes and framed those cat eyes. His body went rigid, his cock filling with a new rush of hot blood as he recalled her wild abandon of not an hour ago. At that very stormy moment, her sweet scent entered his nostrils and enticed him. In response, his mouth watered with the need to taste that hard little knot crowning her pussy.

"Aye, smart for want of a precious coin, I'll give you that, thief. But is he truly *loyal*? When my brother Sheldon arrives offering ten times your bribe, do you really think the lad will remain mum?"

He stopped in his tracks and snarled, "Sheldon will not come near either you or the boy."

"My brother *will* come near me! He will save me from the likes of my beastly kidnapper. Just you wait and see."

"Falcon!"

At the voice, he whirled in the open door of the stable with Salena's inert body tucked snug in his arms. Molly rushed across the muddy ground, a stack of linens and blankets clutched to her ample breasts. He watched as her fiery red hair flowed wet down her back and fluttered behind her in the intermittent light of the night storm. Her black skirts clung to her shapely legs, the fabric plastered against her body by the high winds. He'd had himself buried between those long legs on many an occasion. Oftentimes, he'd detour through these very woods just to get a taste of her, even while in dangerous pursuit by the enemy.

But now...now something was different. The petite body in his arms distracted him somehow. Molly's hair did not appear as silky as before, nor did her tall, voluptuous body seem to draw his eye and make him hunger for her talented charms. Only moments ago on the ride here, he'd longed to slake his lust between her legs this night. But now, now he only desired to cater to the hissing feline pressed warm, small and vulnerable against his chest.

And something quite close to nausea swirled in his gut and made him long to toss the Frost Princess headlong into the turbulent winds and run for his immortal life.

"Falcon?" Molly slowed her steps as she neared and the gleeful smile on her lovely round face faded. "What ails you? And..." Her gaze shifted downward to the bundle in his arms. "Who is that you guard so...so closely?"

The note of jealousy didn't go unnoticed. Something about it made him feel as if she'd just put a noose about his neck and kicked the platform out from beneath his feet.

"Molly." He nodded his greeting. "'Tis Lady Salena Tremayne."

Molly gasped. "Lady Salena Tremayne? Why do you have the future Duchess of Oxford in your company? And holding her in such a...*familiar* manner?"

Her haughty indignation settled much like sour milk in his stomach. "I don't see that it's any of your business, Molly. Now, we need shelter—quickly and discreetly. The lady is drenched and we're both famished."

Molly stepped into the dim interior of the stable and leaned in toward Falcon. Her hot breath swirled out in white puffs of condensation to snare him along with the sharp edge of her tongue. Flashes of lightning lit her angry features and thunder rumbled in the distance, emphasizing her rising ire.

"You dimwit fool! Do you not realize the king will see you beheaded for this? For snatching one of his *prized*—" she sneered it out, " —ladies in waiting?"

"Woman, I'll have you know, I do have a brain within my skull. Now, do you or do you not have shelter for the lady and I?"

Molly's round jaw clamped shut with a clatter. Her nostrils flared while her auburn eyebrows drew together. She spared one more scathing look at Salena. And if looks were lethal, Lady Salena Tremayne would be as dead as the leaves upon the forest floor.

"I do," she said tightly, and spun on her booted heel, her skirts swirling with her anger. He heard a rustle of activity and soon the interior of the large stable glowed by the candle she held in one hand.

"Come this way." She passed through a narrow slat of stalls to a door at the far rear of the barn. Falcon followed her rigid form, the scent of straw and horse now acrid in the air. "The inn is full to capacity, but I do have the tack room available."

She pushed open a rickety wooden door and entered a small room that appeared to be set within the slanted lean-to at the backside of the structure. The aromas of straw, oil and wax rushed into his lungs as he stepped into the low-ceilinged room behind Molly. He glanced about, noting the little stone hearth that filled one short wall, a few logs of firewood and kindling set nearby. Upon the ground across from the hearth, an undressed straw pallet covered the dirt floor. Adjacent to that, in one corner among the various saddles, grooming equipment and shelving, stood a lone chamber pot and close-stool, quite unusual items to be present in a tack room.

Molly tossed the linens and blankets atop the pallet and settled the candle within a round brass candleholder upon the mantel. "I use this room as overflow on rare occasion. Which is why you're afforded some conveniences. But I said rare. Not many, save Lance, his mother and a handful of trusted guests, know of this room." She turned and approached Falcon. The firelight silhouetted her voluptuous body while the shadows seemed to dance upon her face and make her hazel eyes glitter with antipathy. And again, she scrutinized Salena and curled her upper lip with antagonism.

Falcon spoke before she could spew her jealous wrath. "You will be rewarded handsomely, both for your hospitality and your silence." He set Salena down and looked deep into her eyes. Salena glared at him as he ordered, "Remain quiet until after Molly leaves us. In the meantime, go and take the linens and ready the bed for our night's rest."

Falcon dismissed Salena when she stepped over to the mattress and dropped to her knees, immediately obeying him by the powers of his *tazir* spell. But not before he caught the murderous glare in the blue cat's-eye-shaped orbs.

He ignored her and turned back to Molly, addressing her once again. "If you would, send Lance to me. I've something to give him. And please, have him bring along a bite to eat and some additional firewood."

"That's it? Just leave you here with her and send Lance along?"

Falcon sighed and cupped her plump cheek. She groaned with obvious abandonment and pleasure, turning her lips into his palm. His touch could always calm her like a dose of laudanum. He allowed her a moment to nuzzle his hand, surprised when it did nothing to stir him as it might have in the past.

"The lady is in danger, Molly. We must rest and move on by daybreak. I will return soon. I give you my word."

Her eyes turned to limpid pools of relieved surrender. She smiled softly and he experienced a brief stab of regret when she inhaled, presenting him a most tempting, cavernous cleavage. "Ah, I'm pleased to hear you say that." She threw her arms around him, pressing her round breasts into his chest. Out of reflex, he wrapped his arms around her curvy body and smacked her full on the lips.

"And I am pleased with your continued loyalty. Now, we must get dry, warm and nourished."

She groaned her disappointment and stepped away, but her expression no longer reflected distrust or jealousy. That he could always depend on, Molly's understanding of the nature of his business…even if it encompassed having an abducted maiden in his company.

Molly winked. Her voice lowered several smoky octaves as she leaned in toward him. "You're very welcome to warm your cold, weary bones between my bed linens…and my legs."

He chuckled, secretly irritated with himself that the blatant offer hadn't fired up his blood as it normally would have. "I'll certainly keep that in mind."

"Well, you know where my bed is, Falcon Montague." And with that, she blew him a kiss and sashayed from the room.

"Well, you know where my bed is, Falcon Montague."

Salena's mimicking brought him around with a delighted start. Her plump lips were twisted in disgust as she wobbled her head from side to side, imitating Molly's overt invitation.

He chuckled and sauntered toward her. Looking down at her as she struggled to aright a blanket upon the bed, he replied, "Not only is your tongue as sweet and thorny as a rosebush, your servant's talents are sorely lacking."

She came to her feet in the blink of an eye. "I am *not* your servant, you thieving mule's ass!"

And he had her lifted into his arms in yet another blink. "You are as I say, hellcat." Falcon couldn't resist any longer. The urge to claim her mouth once again speared him like a poison-tipped arrow. He knew the consequences, was very aware of how outliving someone you came to adore could be worse than death itself. But this woman had had a hold on his self-control from the moment he'd spied her prim beauty at the jousting tournament. To have saved her to prevent one tragedy had only caused yet another future one, as well as heartache and an endless, lonely immortal life for himself. He now accepted that truth, accepted his temporary fate with this woman.

With one hand, he pressed against the damp cloth over her firm rear so that her pussy ground into his crotch. He could feel the warmth of her skin through the cold thickness of fabric against both his hand and his cock. It tempted him to blinding, maddening distraction. The other hand twined into her long, wet tresses. And with a hunger he'd not experienced in centuries, he forced her mouth to his and attacked, eliciting a gasp from her parted lips.

At that charged, out-of-control moment, Falcon tumbled into blissful insanity.

* * * * *

Salena tasted the flavor of pure danger in his kiss. Even though she silently forbade it, every nerve ending in her body leapt to life. The kiss was clearly one not meant for an innocent. It tempted her as if she were quite the opposite—a shameless harlot. Hesitantly, curious and driven by the pounding between her legs, she parted her lips and let him in. The spear of his tongue—wet and tasting of sinful fruit—hit its target with precise accuracy. It seemed to stab her from her mouth down through her heart, right to her very womb. The damp silk of his tongue chased hers, cloaking it in an erotic dance. She couldn't

move her arms, for he had them pinioned at her sides, but she leaned her body into his, eager to see what lay ahead.

Salena, you idiot! You must stop this madness. You must not encourage this criminal to steal your strength from you.

But all self-scolding fell to the wayside. He suddenly groaned and ground her sensitive area violently against his codpiece. The rough and unexpected movement abraded her juncture over the hardened length of his rod. Salena gasped into his mouth, shocked pleasure bursting through her system. Her clit swelled, throbbing with a need she didn't quite know how to feed. She thought of him touching her on the ride to the inn, the unbelievable pinnacle he'd brought her to… Maybe she could somehow attain similar bliss with this bulging erection just the way the ladies at court whispered about. If she moved her body over his as he'd moved his fingers against her, could she derive the same pleasure right here, at this very moment? It made her wonder…had Thane completely botched her first mating encounter for her? This man here was obviously more skilled at foreplay, which would likely make what followed much more fulfilling. As her first betrothed, she'd fancied Thane to be a master at lovemaking. Salena had experienced vague dissatisfaction and uncertainty back then, true, but now she'd undergone Falcon's phenomenal skill in comparison to Thane's blundering attempts.

Just knowing she had Falcon's amazing talents at her disposal, and contemplating a satisfying coupling caused a rush of sticky wetness to trickle out of her passage and onto her bare inner thighs. It made her hunger for more, enticed her tongue into reciprocation by plunging deep into his mouth. How she suddenly longed to wrap her arms and legs around him, to get closer, to be utterly filled by him!

A knock sounded at the door. Her eyes popped open and she could swear someone had dumped an icy-cold bucket of water over her head. Drowning in mortified devastation, she withdrew her tongue from the hot recesses of his mouth and let out a muffled groan of humiliation.

Harlot! He released her as she silently repeated the insult over and over in her head.

"Nay, not a harlot, love."

She'd forgotten he could read her mind, but there wasn't time to protest. He ran the hot tip of his finger along her jaw and down her neck, stopping only to cup one breast. She sucked in a ragged breath filled with his woodsy scent when he pinched the already hard nipple through the fabric of her nightshift. Fire seemed to race from his wizard's hand and melt every cell between her legs. Her eyelids fluttered, going limp of their own volition.

"You're simply a very passionate maiden trapped inside an amateur's body."

Her eyes flew open. "Get your hands off me." Lord, why did her voice sound so pathetic, as if she didn't mean a word she said?

He threw his head back and roared, the long length of straight, pale hair falling back over his beefy shoulders. "Your words often contradict your thoughts and actions, sweet Salena."

What would it feel like, she wondered, to run her hands through that thick mass of hair? Would she rather do that, or violently pluck every strand from his handsome head?

"Do not poison my given name by using it freely upon your tongue."

"Hmm," he said softly, crossing to the plank door. "As I recall, you rather enjoyed my tongue."

"Oh!" Salena stomped one booted foot on the dirt floor and folded her arms over her midriff. "You are *the* most insufferable oaf I've ever had the misfortune of meeting."

"Fortune, misfortune…" He shrugged and reached for the iron handle. "From my point of view, you've been quite profitable…or will be." And he cupped his erection to emphasize his point.

She ground her teeth together and growled in frustration as he swung the door open. *Pompous ass!*

"I heard that," he threw over his shoulder with a warning tone. To Lance he said as he stepped aside to allow him entry, "You are prompt, dependable and very loyal. The very makings of a Merry Gentleman."

Lance beamed as he carried in a basket of foodstuff. He seemed not to care or notice that Falcon hid behind a coward's mask.

"You really think so, sir? Do you think someday, I can ride with you and your men?" By the light of the lone candle, Lance's damp midnight hair gleamed with bluish streaks. He set the basket upon the hearth, bustled back to the door for an armload of wood and stacked it neatly with the other logs. Immediately, he arranged kindling and twigs in a pile inside the hearth. Obviously well practiced in flames and his expected duties, he had the fire sparking in seconds.

"Oh, with all my soul, lad." With that, Falcon added a wink and took several moments to root through his gunnysack. Finally, he added, "And here's the proof of my confidence in you."

The boy's grin faded when Falcon held up a gold coin. It twinkled and glimmered by the light of the fireplace. Falcon's gaze moved back and forth between Lance and the coin in his own hand. He wiggled his fingers, rolling the coin's edge over knuckles, fingertips, palm. The round disc seemed to enthrall the boy far more than Falcon's own spells had captured Salena.

"Is it mine?" Lance tossed a larger log onto the fire and walked slowly up to Falcon. His head tipped back, he looked up, watching every suave move the thief made.

"Aye, yours for all your hard work and allegiance." With that, he tossed the coin upward so that it toppled through the air. It glittered with flashes of gold on its way down, and landed perfectly within Falcon's palm. He extended his hand. "Go ahead. Take it. 'Tis yours, lad."

Lance snatched it, his eyes bulging as he held it up to examine its smooth surface. Next, he bit into it, testing its authenticity. Salena's heart did an involuntary flip at both the boy's reaction and the tender generosity of the man who had caused it.

"Mine…"

"Yours. And this one," Falcon said, drawing another to the boy's attention, "is your ma's. Give it to her, Lance, and tell her a stranger from afar sends his condolences for your pa's untimely death at the king's hand."

Lance looked up then, his dark eyes glistening with tears, and choked out, "Thank you." He knelt and threw his arms around one of Falcon's thick legs. His gaze rose to capture Falcon's surprised one. "You are forever in my prayers, kind sir. I will never forget your generosity…" He grinned and added, "Robin Hood."

Falcon chuckled. "Oh, aye, Robin Hood, that I am, the pilfering thief, the bloody murderer. Now, up on your feet, boy."

Lance rose and Falcon dropped the second gold coin into the lad's hand. "Be gone with you. But first, go and snatch one of those tiny loaves of bread and a hunk of cheese from the basket you've just brought. Take it with you for you and your ma. I'd like to see a bit more meat on your bones and a few inches to grow on, the next time I pass through these woods."

Salena's breath fluttered in her chest when Lance grinned, tears still brimming his eyes. He crossed to the hearth, chose the food offered and returned to the door.

"Thank you," Lance whispered, and tucked the coins into a tiny leather pouch at his hip.

"Thank *you*." Falcon patted his head and ruffled the thick, damp hair. "Now, be off. And remember, mum's the word."

"Aye, I promise with my life, sir!" And he was gone.

Falcon closed the portal and latched it. Turning, he said with a rasp, "Let's see, now…where were we?"

Still in shock from that hypnotizing display of ogre-turned-kind-prince, Salena had to take a minute to clear her head. But now she saw the ogre was back—with a vengeance if the arrogant, stalking swagger were any indication. Still somewhat restricted but for the orders he'd given her to make the bed, she leaned back to avoid his advance, her feet planted in place against her will. The defensive move made her fall backward atop the pallet. Her cloak gaped open revealing the nightgown beneath its thickness.

"My, but you're a clumsy one. Always falling, it seems." He knelt near the mattress and climbed toward her, the panther stalking his wounded prey.

"Nay, villain. Not falling, but attempting to escape the clutches of a dangerous crook." She tried to replace the cloak over her chest and legs. But it was no use. There seemed to be no rhyme or reason for her abilities to move or not—except that this cunning warlock was apparently hard at work allowing it one moment, forbidding it the next. At times she could move, and yet at others, her limbs seemed completely paralyzed.

He now perched over her on all fours. She looked up into eyes already glazed with mischief and mayhem to come. Her blood thudded painfully at every pulse point in her body. She could smell the wild scent of him, the damp peril simmering beneath the outdoorsy, pleasant scent. Her mouth went dry when he smiled wickedly, his eyes narrowing into twin emeralds as they stared back at her through the slits of the mask he still wore.

"Mm, dangerous." He said it with an oddly agreeable tone as he lowered his mouth to hers. Flames of pleasure raced through her body from her lips to the very tips of her toes. He dragged his mouth back and forth over hers, the warmth and softness so in contrast to the murderous gleam in his eyes and the hard body that threatened to crush her.

She turned her face to the side. "Don't."

He turned her face back to him. Against her mouth, he whispered, "Do."

"I-I can't do this. I…I can't kiss a stranger."

He pressed his lips together attempting to suppress a grin. "You've already done so, madam. And besides, I'd say, given our prior acquaintance—however miniscule—at court and our prior intimacy, I'm no longer a stranger."

She pointedly ignored that last remark. "No. I mean… Remove the mask—please."

Except for the crackle of the small logs catching to the flame in the hearth, silence ensued. He stared into her eyes for the longest time, as if he warred with some personal decision.

Unable to remove her gaze from his, she held her breath when he reached up and swiped the black mask from his face.

And Salena would never, in all of her days, forget the sight that met her eyes.

Chapter Four

"What's the matter, love? Snarling tiger got your tongue?"

"Please...please give me permission to touch you."

His eyes twinkled with both satisfaction and sorcery. "You may move all of your body—if it means that you will grace me with your tender touch. And remember, Salena, as always, it is your choice on how far to take matters...but you are forbidden to alert passersby with your screams."

Her arms, torso and legs tingled immediately following the glowing beams from his eyes. As if she were his servant, she'd been ordered by his powers to make the bed. It had left her limbs in a state of dormancy once the task had been completed. Free now of the spell, she lifted one trembling hand and traced the huge gash that trailed from the left side of his forehead, down over the temple and cheek to the front of his ear. It felt bumpy against her fingertips, yet the raw edges were smooth and white in comparison to his tawny skin. He hissed in a breath when she pinched it, as if to close the opening to return him to normal. It appeared to be a fairly fresh wound, perhaps less than half a fortnight old.

"W-what happened? How...how did you get this horrible injury?"

He reached for her hand and planted a kiss in the palm. It made her think of Molly nuzzling his hand, and a strange, fierce sense of covetousness reared up to provoke her. But that was utterly ridiculous! Yes, she pitied this man and his disfigurement, but she most certainly couldn't care one whit if he charmed or even bedded another woman.

Oh, but her stomach jumped with an odd swirl of something very much like that feeling when he'd touched her...down there! His tongue danced around her flesh sending shivers up her arm and into her breasts. He drew one of her fingers into his mouth and she nearly came off the mattress with a choked cry of ecstasy. Gooseflesh quickly ignited into an inferno, settling heavy and hot into her pussy.

Around her finger, as he twirled his tongue and sucked her resolve right from her soul, he spoke with a huskiness that affected her in much the same manner. "How did I become so ugly, you ask? Why, by the perils of illegal thieving, of course."

She caught the sarcasm in his tone, but by now, he had her in a fog of eroticism she could not push her way out of. "You are not—" she gasped when his free hand moved down to drag her gown up, "—ugly by any means." She pushed the gown back into place.

He lifted his head then, and stared into her eyes with an almost boyish uncertainty and wonder. "You jest."

"Nay." A brief moment of pity—or was it tenderness?—washed through her. She couldn't resist holding his jaw so that the tips of her fingers touched just below the jagged edges of the wound. "Despite the horrible look of the injury itself, you are, I must regrettably admit, quite breathtakingly handsome—for a criminal, that is."

"Of course, as thieves go, I'm quite sought after," he said with a snarl. His tone jolted her from that dangerous cloud of reverie. As did his touch. That hot hand returned to the hem of her gown and slid the fabric up the front of her thighs.

As a result, she didn't have time to give him a biting retort to that remark. In fact, her well-chosen repartee turned to sudden mush within her brain...right along with the mushy ache that settled in her core.

"Don't." She shoved the fabric down so that her legs were covered once again. Ah, but it took every ounce of strength to do so, to deny herself the pleasure of his scalding touch.

He sighed as if she completely bored him. "You will get out of these wet clothes, Lady Salena, if I have to *tazir* you into it."

She blinked. "You are a tyrant, a monster."

"So be it, but nonetheless—" he blew out on a long breath, "—you will disrobe this very moment. We must depart by daybreak. You will then need a warm, dry cloak. And your garments *will* be dry enough by then to place in my bag and exchange with new ones. That, my love, is a definite fact."

"Oh!" She growled it out, sitting up with jerky, irritated movements. He rolled onto his back allowing her a brief respite of freedom. "Then impart me some gentlemanly privacy and turn your bloody back to me. And do *not* call me your 'love' ever again!"

The laugh came out as a deep rumble that grated on her nerves. "Silly, you are. I turn my back only to turn yet again and see you nude, anyway? You've no fresh clothes at hand, it seems, my dear."

"No, you get me a clean, dry change of garments from your bag of stolen bounty, and I don them and go to sleep."

"No, I do not."

She stared agog at him, trying her best to ignore the bunching of his arm muscles as he laced his hands behind his head. Cocky. He was the most arrogant, cocky bastard she'd ever had the misfortune of meeting. Oh, but that hard body of his! She struggled to keep her traitorous gaze from moving down over the huge, taut frame...down to that bulge that pressed against the backside of his codpiece. Salena nearly let out a groan when her passage wetted with a hot, sticky fluid.

"Why are you doing this to me?" Her voice sounded desperate to her own ears, and it made her hate him all the more for this strange, magical control he had over her.

He sat up slow and deliberate. His eyes snared her before she had a chance to escape them. That shimmering sensation of his powers—almost like the pinnacle of bliss he'd shown her earlier—oozed into her system.

"Because it is for your own good that I do not wish you to be stricken with illness. Now, you will rise, remove the gown, place it by the hearth and return to me here in the bed. And we will make love just as you wish to do deep down, but cannot admit to yourself. That is, we will if it is your choice."

"No…" she whispered, tears stinging her eyes.

Yes! Her mind shouted out the contradiction. It was as if two people resided in her mind, screaming at one another in constant opposition.

"Must I also take your voice from you, Salena?"

She shook her head. "No. I wish to at least be able to tell you how much I hate you as you force yourself upon me."

His expression didn't so much as flinch. "You can tell me you hate me all you want. You can tell me no, as well. You can deny that you want me with your voice. But we both know you only deceive yourself—do not forget I can hear your thoughts. And we both know, as well, that it will not ever be forced between us, but a fiery, passionate mating that will meld our souls into one. Yes, it is ultimately your choice whether or not you welcome me between your legs. I never have and never will force my powers upon a woman to conquer her. It never has been necessary. And this case is no different…since it is apparent your wanton soul will prevail over your prim façade of propriety."

Salena warred simultaneously with the hate that filled her heart and desire. It was simply alarming how easily he could ignite passion in her by his mere words. There was no eluding him, no eluding herself. In spite of her morals, of her almost-virginal state, she wanted this man to show her the delights of the flesh. She'd wanted it, she suddenly realized with shocking honesty, from the first moment she'd glimpsed him at the king's tournament. Most certainly, she'd taken leave of her emotional senses since she'd been assaulted by the sight of him kneeling on her bed in her chamber. Deep down, she'd seen herself there with him instantly, rolling across the bed, locked in a fiery embrace she never wished to be set free from.

So why fight a battle she could not win?

The internal admission stunned her, yet it made it all the easier for her to rise and go to the fireplace. Her movements were slow, perfunctory. She ceased her steps and stared at the small stone mantel, wondering how one dull, ordinary night in her chambers had come to this, to a wanton surrendering to a thief, to her handsome, ruthless captor. Yes, she had the option to say no, and she somehow trusted that he would honor her wishes. But the combat with her own curiosity and depravity proved more futile than battling even the weakest of his sorcerer's spells.

And so, with her back to him, she slowly untied her cloak and pushed it from her shoulders. Unhurriedly, almost sensuously, she laid it across the stone rise before the fire. Next came the nightrail and boots. The swish of the damp fabric preceded the sudden heat of the fire on her naked skin...and the heat of his gaze upon her bare backside.

Already, her nipples stood in tight anticipation, while her clitoris engorged and pulsed with an aching sensation that took her breath from her lungs. Her heart thumped wildly, and she wondered if she'd still have the will to surrender if he hadn't cast his powers over her. Yes, the ultimate choice was hers, but for now, he continued to wield his authority over her just to see her dry and safe from illness.

Would she have disrobed from the damp clothing if not for his forced, magical order to do so? For the love of England, surely not! She could still want him, fantasize about him, but she'd never have willingly rendered herself vulnerable and given in to him if it weren't for this wicked, carnal sorcery he wielded over her. But that small bit of self-assurance dissolved through the sieve of his next command, one accompanied by the tingle of release of the spell. No longer under his powers, it *was* now her choice. God, how she suddenly longed for the spell to claim her again, to give her the excuse to salvage her reputation and pride!

"Turn around."

Drawing in a bout of courage, she inhaled the oddly pleasing aroma of smoke mixed with the food in the basket Lance had brought. But bravery was useless, she realized. Her traitorous body, as if still under his magic, did not seem to care what fears or excuses her mind insisted on. Closing her eyes, she gathered her courage and turned around to face him, her body trembling, her womb contracting against the flames of anticipation that ignited there.

He hissed out a lungful of air followed by a moan. "Salena... Open your eyes. You know you are free to do as you please...or not."

Her eyelids fluttered open while her heart pounded against her breastbone. She couldn't breathe, couldn't think, not with his gaze devouring her as he stroked his long, thick cock with one hand. The dirt floor chilled her feet as she moved barefoot across the room toward him, heedless to the fact that she'd gone to him and obeyed without being told. Something drove her, something wicked and licentious within her soul, far more powerful than his supernatural abilities.

Salena's gaze lowered slow and dreamlike until it fell upon his hard, flexed bulk. He'd apparently removed all of his clothing at the very moment she had disrobed, for he now lay naked across the blankets, the firelight dancing upon his body. The sight of his tan, muscled flesh made her mouth water. Her pussy soaked with reluctant yet eager desire for the act to come, and she hoped it would be a far better experience than the first had been with Thane.

She clenched her fists, itching to run her palms down the rippled wall of his lightly hairy chest, taking comfort in the fact that Thane had never moved her to such desires. Instead, her gaze moved lower, down over the tight abdomen, down to the veiny protrusion jutting from a bed of golden curls. At court, she'd heard whisperings of how a man's tool could please a woman. Visions of that very large penis buried between her legs made her all but swoon. A heaviness filled her labia, nipples, nub and passage all at once. Tightening her groin muscles, she struggled to hold the flood of wetness within her.

Yes, there was no doubt about it. She wanted this man to take her, no matter the consequences that may arise in her engagement to another. But wanting something and actually *doing* it were two entirely different concepts.

"You've been released. Your body is free of the wet garments and safe from possible illness. Now you may do as you wish, dove."

It didn't surprise her that he'd released her. She knew that he was aware of her thoughts, her every yearning. He knew that, for the moment, she was his and would not be attempting to flee. Even if she tried to do so, he'd be after her in a flash, dragging her back to face her newly born demons. So she chose the less tumultuous route and gave herself up to the inevitable. Her heart galloped into her throat, choking her with excitement when she knelt with her knee next to his bare hip. The warmth he exuded against her leg further seduced her to him, making her long to throw herself upon the blazing mass of his body.

He reached up and drew her mouth down to his. "Ah, beautiful princess...kiss me. Give me what I know your heart requests."

As if his powers were still in force over her body, she suddenly collapsed across his chest. She marveled at the strength and power of his body. The solid heat of him permeated her chilled flesh, and his manhood pressed hard and thick into her abdomen. Delicious, irresistible sensations bombarded her from every angle, heightening each of her senses to an almost unbearable level. She could smell his woodsy scent, feel his warm breath upon her cheek, almost taste the flavor of him without even touching her mouth to his.

"But I do not know what to do, Falcon. It's only been...once. You already know that I'm somewhat..."

"Inexperienced? Yes, but inexperienced innocents can still have desires." He stroked her hair, tucking it behind her ear when a thick strand fell across his cheek. "Tell this thief of your wanton desires, Salena, so that I may take them from you, mold them to your needs and gift them back to you…so that you will never forget me."

She swallowed a lump in her throat when his hands slid down her back to cup her buttocks. It made her gasp out her words. "I want you…to make me feel the way you did…on our journey here."

"Ah," he rasped, moving his hand up and around to mold one of her breasts in his palm. Her throaty pants became ragged and an inferno ignited in her nipple. She nearly screamed out her pleasure when he hitched her up and took it into his mouth, speaking around the taut bud as he slathered his tongue over it. "You want to reach climax, is that right?"

"Yes…" she whimpered, struggling to keep her eyes open. He sucked the nipple into his mouth and lightly clamped his teeth over it. And she almost reached that sought-after pinnacle at that very moment. "Yes!"

He dragged her up further so her vee barely touched the tip of his rod. She was already so sticky, the movement made her lips part. And her clit pulsed, engorging anew with a delicious, heavy flood of desire.

"Go ahead." His voice was strained, his eyes limpid pools of passion. He closed his large hands over her hips and danced her body over his, showing her, teaching her what to do. "Rub yourself over me. Pleasure yourself. Become accustomed to its— ah!—size and feel."

Each time he moved her upward, the head of his shaft grazed her knot, flicking over it until it settled at the opening of her vagina. And each time she whimpered as her loins grew hot with insistent need. Slowly gaining her bravery, Salena planted her hands beside his head. She looked down into his eyes and watched, totally captivated as he folded his hands behind his head and merely looked up at her from hooded, dangerous eyes.

"Yes, that's right, darling," he coaxed, his voice strained. "Allow yourself to use it as a gratification tool."

"I...I'm getting you all wet." The words came out from between clenched teeth, and her face warmed at her own boldness.

He dragged in a breath. "You're supposed to get me all wet, sweetheart. It will make the joining so much more pleasant, believe me."

"Joining..." The word had the effect of a flame bursting between her legs. She could smell her own arousal now mingled with his manly scent. The only sounds were those of the crackling fire, the pitter-patter of rain upon the small window across the room, the rumble of far-off thunder and their erratic breathing. As she moved in a circular motion, shyly rubbing her vee against his erection, her nipples dragged and scraped alternately over the stubble on his jaw and the hair upon his chest. The maddening sensations of it all made her shiver, and a moan escaped her pursed lips. He reached out and yanked a blanket over her back, as if he assumed the shivering had been due to cold.

But that was the farthest thing from the truth. Her entire insides combusted with a hot need she couldn't quite slake, couldn't quite quench.

"I-I...please, Falcon. Show me how. I...I need to feel it again."

He groaned as if he were about to die and rose up, turning her so that she now lay on her back. Poised above her, his long, pale hair glistening in the firelight, he brought to mind a fierce and mighty Viking warrior, a man of deadly intent prepared to pillage and cast mayhem on all in his path. Her heart did a quick skip then a surging, painful beat. Ah, but he simply took her breath away!

"My lady, my Salena, I must have you. Forgive me, but there is no way about it. No way for me to turn back now." He forced her legs apart with one muscular thigh and moved until his hips settled there instead. The naughty sensation of it made her reach up and around so that she clung to his shoulders. Now desperate to experience that delicious sensation once again, she spread her legs wider.

"Nor for me. Show me. Now." She raced her hands down over the tense and corded muscles of his back. "Gift me with that delicious bliss once again. Just this once…"

His mouth covered hers, so tender and gentle compared to the fierce aggression that glittered in his eyes. She tasted of him, arching her back when his hand found her wetness. He pushed a finger through the curls of her apex, finding the treasure of her womanhood. Her clit now swollen and aching with need, seemed to cry out its own demands. Falcon flickered his thumb over its hardness, swirling around the small mass until she screamed into his mouth. His tongue dipped between her lips at the precise moment he sank a finger in her pussy. Slowly, almost lovingly, he buried the finger to the tops of his knuckles, and Salena heard a rush of blood in her ears. Honey poured onto his hand. One by one, he added another finger, then another.

"Ah, I believe you're quite ready now." His hoarse voice captivated her, made her hunger for that mouth on hers again.

She reached up and held his face in her hands, careful not to further injure the slashing wound. It was at that moment when she looked deep into the gems of his eyes, that she knew her world had changed forever. How, she couldn't quite put into words, but there was no denying it. The sight of him just now, his hair all askew, his lips swollen and moist, his eyes burning with an unknown, disturbing emotion…it all foretold of danger and life-altering events down an entirely different path than she'd planned for herself.

Plans of only hours ago.

The realization almost brought her to her feet, almost forced her to flee out into the dark of night as far from this wicked bandit as possible. But it seemed she paused a split second too long. He reached for her hands, drew them up next to her ears and held them down against the pallet. And he pushed his enormous cock into her depths.

* * * * *

Falcon saw what he thought was a brief flicker of panic in her eyes. It quickly turned to a glazed, lustful look. But there was no way he could stop himself, no way he could take the time to further explore it. He just could not deny either of them the pleasure to come any longer.

The tightness of her pussy made him sigh yet he paused, holding firm to rigid restraint in order to allow her time to adjust to his size. She gasped and stiffened, but when he gentled his movements, she relaxed a small measure and he felt her legs slacken and widen further.

Ah, but she was so very snug, so hot and sticky inside!

"Oh…" she rasped, her chest rising and falling in rapid succession against his own. "It-it hurt a bit at first b-but it feels so good now. I feel it, I feel that delicious sensation again, just out of reach."

Her body lay small and feminine beneath his, begging for the dominance of man, of a firm hand. He stretched her arms further above her head holding her captive by the wrists, forcing her breasts upward until the jewels of her nipples puckered enticingly.

"Salena, love…" He kissed her tasting wild abandon and needy desire. Her lips were warm and sweet against his, but there was nothing innocent about the way she began to gently buck her hips upward. "You will be the death of me, to be sure."

"Yes, you will die for this, for abducting me, for taking me captive. The king will see to that. But for now…just kiss me and give me that feeling again. *Please*." She said those last contradictory words with a pleading, hoarse tone. Combined with her thorny words, the song of her sexy voice made him wild with the need to reach an end.

"If it comforts you to think so, Lady Tremayne, then so be it." And with that, he rammed himself into her until his balls slapped against her ass. She screamed, and if not for the enthusiastic rise of her own hips to meet his, he would have thought he'd hurt her. In a wild frenzy, she yanked her arms free and raked her nails down his back. The pleasant pain of it intensified his own longing. His cock surged with an aching rush, the sac swelled, nearly bursting each time it came into contact with the round mounds of her rear.

She moaned and groaned, tossing her head from side to side. "Yes, oh, yes! I'm almost there again!"

Falcon had never experienced such surrender, such tight silk wrapped about his cock. True, this was his very first inexperienced woman, but no one could compare to her, no matter the depth of talent. Salena's pussy drove him to an abyss of madness he feared he'd never crawl out of. Her rosy scent mixed with the smells of sex and perspiration wafted up to tempt him. He rocked his pelvis, driving himself into her slick canal time and time again. With each penetration, she moaned louder, clutching at him, her legs wrapping around his waist. Finally, he had no choice but to silence her. Fear of being heard by passersby or patrons of the inn forced him to slam his mouth against hers and drink of her vocal growls.

Her tongue darted between his lips forcing his clamped teeth apart. She sucked his tongue into her mouth, swirling, drinking, dancing in a seductive move that left him breathless. The sensation of it moved in a ferocious, tingly wave straight from his tongue to his tortured shaft.

God, but I must have release soon!

As if the thought made it so for both of them, she tore her mouth from his and stilled her movements. He looked down into her glazed eyes, almost navy by the light of the fire. The pupils were dilated as if she'd been given a massive dose of opium. Her mouth fell open and she sucked in a gasp at the exact moment he spilled his seed into her. Ecstasy washed through him and he groaned, but he forced himself to keep his eyes open so he could watch her. She jerked, her eyelids fluttered and her pussy muscles spasmed around his still-spewing cock. Salena milked him of more cum, drawing out the climax. The feel of it coupled with the beautiful, surprised expression, the limpid cat eyes...it stole his heart from his very chest.

"Falcon..." she whimpered. "Falcon."

"Yes, I know, Salena. I know." He sighed and gathered her close until her body relaxed. For a long moment, they held one another, their breathing slowing, their hearts calming.

Exhaustion began to overtake him, and he slowly slipped from her passage, hissing at the sudden rush of cold air against his wet cock. Salena lay still staring up at the ceiling. If not for the rise and fall of her chest, he'd have thought her dead.

"Get some sleep, princess," he whispered, nipping at her lobe.

She shrugged him away and turned her back to him, but not before he saw the lone tear in one eye. He clamped his eyes tight against the sudden guilt that washed over him. *No, Falcon*, he thought. *It was inevitable. And she wanted it just as much as you did. She'd given in of her own free will without the use of your powers.*

He tucked the blankets around them and gathered her close, ignoring the stiffening of her limbs, the gradual vibration of one stifling the wrath of tears. It was to the feel of her warm, regretful body tucked into the curve of his own that he drifted off to sleep.

Until the sharp rap on the door brought him out of sweet dreams of a sable-haired, passionate maiden and into a nightmare.

Chapter Five

Cradled in the clutches of slumber, Salena heard the soft yet insistent pounding from afar. It turned into the dreamy clip-clop of a horse's gait upon hard ground. She drifted in a mist the very color of his eyes. At every turn, the masked bandit was there, grabbing at her, snatching her up and onto his sleek black Friesian stallion. Sitting astride the beast and at Falcon's back, she clung to his strong torso as he whirled Warrior about, facing her angry brother.

Sheldon circled them, perched proud upon his own mount. She gasped at the murderous gleam in his dark eyes. His shoulder-length, red hair blew about his sharp-featured face. From across the distance, she could almost smell the acrid odor of his ire mixed with the scent of coming rain.

"Salena, come home," he roared, his voice echoing in her head as he spurred his horse closer. "You harlot! The Duke of Oxford will never marry you now. Come home, Salena…"

She saw the sword in his hand too late. With a heinous cackle, Sheldon darted forward, his rapier aimed for Falcon's chest. Salena looked down in horror, screaming when the blade missed its intended target and plunged into her abdomen. She gasped as the sharp pain of it pierced her, plunging through her body and exiting near her spine. Blood spewed forth. She was suddenly cold, so very cold.

Falcon cursed. All she could see and hear was Falcon as he gripped her shoulders and kept her from falling off the horse. There was so much blood…

"Salena." He shook her. Slumber ebbed from her groggy mind. "Salena! You must awaken."

She gulped in air, certain a lung had been penetrated. "Oh, God, help me!" Her throat was dry and scratchy. She forced her eyelids open. "Falcon?"

He came into focus, the small stable room they'd bedded down in surrounding him. Ah, thank the Lord, she'd been dreaming. Salena sighed, steadying her rapid pulse. She pressed a shaky hand to her belly, only now calming. The imagined pain inflicted by her brother now drifted back into the realm of sleep where it belonged. The frightening experience had been nothing more than a dream. Cold horror faded and she embraced the chill of the room, a space that now felt safe…like a haven from the outside world.

"Yes, it's your one and only brigand. Now, you must rise and get dressed. 'Tis time to flee to safety."

"Get dressed? Flee to safety? B-but—"

"Woman, there is no time for arguments. Your life depends upon your haste." He dragged her from the bed, a blanket wrapped about her body. "Don your garments this instant!"

Across the small distance in the room, only embers remained in the hearth. And Lance stood at the door pale-faced. His eyes bulged at the sight of her being snatched from her bed…naked.

Embarrassment took second place to satisfying her curiosity. "What's going on?" Her stare settled on Falcon who'd already turned to busy himself with their departure. "I demand to know this instant what has caused you to awaken me from a much-needed rest and command me to rise before I'm ready." Neither Lance nor Falcon seemed to put forth rationalizations for this abrupt activity, therefore, she would demand them before moving even one inch—brutish rogue or not.

"Master Sheldon has arrived. He is in a foul mood," Lance finally offered.

She whipped her head around to snare Lance with her hungry gaze. Her eyes flared. Hope bloomed in her chest...along with a curious undertone of disappointment she didn't care to examine. "My brother has come for me?"

"He may have come for you," Falcon said as he hurriedly gathered up their belongings and shoved them into his bag. "But he's not going to get you." His glittering green eyes fell upon her, making her shiver with trepidation and something altogether volatile that she didn't care to examine.

"I'll decide if I'd like to go home with my brother or not!"

"Lance, leave us and ready my mount, boy." His voice came out low, ominous. Salena shivered when he reached into the bag, drew out a silver coin and tossed it to the boy, all without taking those glaring eyes from her. "And not a word, you hear?"

Lance snatched the coin in midair and grinned. "Aye, sir." And he was gone.

"Bribery. You can add that to your list of offenses to be hanged for." She crossed her arms tight over her midriff, holding the quilt in place.

But apparently, it was too late. He had her enthralled. The beams from his eyes zapped her so fast she didn't even have time to blink.

"You will get dressed now with these." He reached into the bag and drew out one of her gardening gowns and underthings. "And quickly. Next you will don your boots and your cloak— with the hood over your head and face. Quietly, without making one sound or alerting Sheldon or any of his consorts in any manner, you will follow me posthaste to where Lance has Warrior awaiting us. We will mount and leave without so much as a footprint left behind. Do you understand me?"

Her body leapt into obedience mode, but even as her limbs did his bidding, her mouth protested. "Oh, yes, I understand that I hate you. You cannot *do* this to me!" She drew the undergarments and fresh gown over her head and settled them into place. "My own loving brother has come to rescue me—he must be worried sick by now! And yet you're still bent on continuing with this murder-plot farce? Well, I ask you, *who better to turn me safely over to than my own brother?* Falcon, I'm speaking to you!"

When he remained silent and continued readying their belongings, she knew that very farce to be nothing more than an excuse to abduct a wealthy lady—and to have his way with her. Why else would he not hand her over to her own flesh and blood?

She went on, determined to have her say before he stole her voice from her. "Well, you may have taken advantage of me that one regrettable time, thief, and it's unfortunate for me that you have obvious and unfair possession of my body at your own selfish will. But be forewarned. You can order my body about all you want, but you can never have my heart, mind or soul. I will fight you to the bitter end."

He snatched up the mask where it still lay near the pallet. Jamming it down over his head, he stared at her once again through the slits. The lover with the tender, magic touch of last night had disappeared and in his place, the cruel marauder had returned.

"Taken advantage of?" He snorted. "I think not. You eagerly surrendered of your own volition, Lady Salena. And you say loving brother, eh? Well, we shall see about that. And we shall see about that icy heart, mind and soul of yours, as well."

"Oh!" Salena longed to cover her ears. Lord help her, but she didn't wish to hear his cruel reminder of her shocking behavior. She plopped down upon the mattress and watched as her own hands submissively placed her boots on her feet. With the task swift and complete, she rose and donned her cloak, tossing the hood over her head as ordered. "You are an insufferable—"

"Pompous ass," he finished. She shivered when his eyes snared her with further power. He settled the bag and longbow across his back. "Milady, you will not speak another word until I give you permission. You will accompany me as I've already ordered. Do what you may to keep yourself warm and such, but you will stay with me and not flee or alert anyone of our whereabouts. Now, we must depart."

With the prudence of a practiced criminal, he slowly opened the door and peered out into the early morning darkness of the open stable. From afar she could hear the neighing of horses, the alarming tone of men's shouts carrying upon the damp dawn air. Mixed in with the bark of orders and the whistle of the wind, she heard Sheldon's voice.

Guilt clutched at her stomach. He'd obviously been running the search party all night, worried sick over her welfare, frantic and scared of what may have come of her. And all the while she'd been bedding the enemy. Nausea spiraled through her system. *Harlot!*

"Nay, not a harlot. Hardly that," Falcon added under his breath. And he reached for her hand. Closing his big one over hers, heat suffused up her fingers and into her arm. He tugged her along, ducking behind straw piles and stalls. They slipped out a rear door to where Lance waited with Warrior.

The sky above remained dark and starless, the storm having left behind a gray cloud of gloom. But the horizon was just beginning to alight with deep pink and orange streaks, teasing but not promising a respite. The rain had stopped, yet the atmosphere felt bathed with its cool humidity, while the scent of more coming rain hovered drearily about. A chill wrought the air, making Salena draw her cloak tighter against her body.

She darted her eyes all around, starving for the sight of Sheldon. Her body continued to follow dutifully behind Falcon, but her mind screamed for her brother to happen upon them and rescue her from this bizarre and shameful kidnapping. True, Sheldon's plans for her to marry were now ruined. Word would get out that she'd been abducted by the infamous rogue Robin Hood…which, by the sheer nature of his reputation, meant she'd already been torn down from society's pedestal.

And by mere association, it went unsaid that she'd been deflowered—whether she had or not.

But her dear brother would not reject her. He'd see that her reputation was restored. He'd find her a suitable match if the duke refused to take her to wife. If only she could fight this spell and shout to alert him. Or command her legs to carry her right into the safety of her brother's caring embrace. Only she knew it wasn't to be, not at least, at the moment. Sheldon would find her eventually, she thought as Falcon lifted her up onto the steed's back. No amount of magic could keep her from returning to the safety of her beloved home.

Lance waved and disappeared through the stable door without a word.

Falcon swung up onto the horse behind her, drawing her body against the wall of his chest. "We ride now," he whispered, sending a shiver through her chilled body. "What I'll do with you when we get there, however, is beyond me."

I will escape you. That I vow with every breath I take.

He whirled Warrior around and took off into a dense section of the copse behind the barn. The sounds of Sheldon's rescue party gradually faded, and with it, her heart sank.

"If it makes you feel better to believe so, my fiery wench, please do indulge. But I can think of other more interesting ways to treat yourself…" He pulled her snug against him. Warmth enveloped her and she caught the earthy scent of him upon the breeze.

Keep your thieving hands off me!

He sighed. A hand came up to delve into the opening of her cloak. He nestled his palm across her quivering abdomen. "'Tis no use, little dove. Your mind reasons away what your body demands—of its own needs, without the influence of my *tazir* powers. You know it. I know it."

Bastard.

He chuckled, apparently encouraged rather than dissuaded by her silent vehemence.

As they trotted along placing miles between them and the inn, they darted through underbrush and around massive oaks and maples. An uneventful, silent hour passed in which they partook of the bread, cheese and wine Lance had provided for them. The danger of being discovered was now long gone...and his hand slipped into her bodice making firm contact with her flesh. She gasped, astounded that her body could come to life with such quick, agile traitorousness. There was no possible way she could ignore the swift onslaught of lust that curled deep into her abdomen when his adept fingers found her already taut nipple.

No...

"Yes." He pinched the knot, and she could have sworn he struck up a flame and held it to her areola. Visions of their mating only hours past filled her mind. She could recall with vivid clarity the flood of wetness between her thighs, the sensation of his huge organ filling her, stretching her tender pussy. Just thinking about it caused sticky juice to pour from her core in a shocking gush. She closed her eyes, damning herself for her continued weakness, yet welcoming the carnal web he weaved around her, into her. Her head fell back against his chest in abandon.

"I want you again, Salena." His words sounded ragged and strained, as if just to speak pained him. It made her shiver, made her eyelids flutter shut and her heart beat erratically. "But, as usual, this aspect of our acquaintance is not under the blanket of my spells. It is your decision once again."

Ah, you want me again. Well, that is no secret. And obviously, I cannot hide my thoughts from you, either, so I'll admit to a reluctant want, as well. But hear this, wizard ravager. You can steal my family's trinkets, and a bauble or coin here and there. And now it seems, you're able to take my own desires and turn them into some sort of dark, erotic force against me. But again, Robin Hood, Prince of Plunderers, you can never have my heart or soul.

He growled. "You present a challenge I cannot resist conquering." He yanked her around to face him, even as the horse continued on its journey. Angered by her impassioned vow, he forced her legs apart so that she faced him, straddling him as they rode. The move drew her skirts up to her calves, and biting-cold air swirled up into the folds of her gown. She welcomed the coolness, sighed when it caressed her scorching mons.

"You may move your entire body now in whatever fashion you wish except escape. A decision made because I desire to feel your arms around me, the unbridled movements of that passion of yours you keep under discriminate lock and key. And I want to feel you clutch desperately at me when I shove this—" he slammed her pussy against his codpiece, "—into your sweet depths."

She gasped, a warm throbbing ache settling into her core. "I...oh, God, what sort of sorcery have you wielded over me? Why is it that even void of your powers, my body continues to disobey me?"

He shoved her skirts up. "Because of this." Salena looked down between her legs, as did Falcon. His green eyes glazed over with a rabid need that further enflamed her. Just then, the sun peeped through a hole in the gray morning clouds. A lone ray of sunlight shone upon her glistening pearl. The scent of her arousal wafted up to tease her, to make her forget her need to escape this villain. All she could think of was achieving that new climactic bliss this man had introduced her to. It seemed he'd enticed her into an addiction she could not control, despite her perilous situation. She needed it, had to have it before her cunt imploded.

"And because of this..." Chest rising and falling with a rapid rhythm, he freed his tool from behind the layer of his codpiece and braies. By the light of the sun, a white droplet of wetness glistened upon its tip. She'd never before seen a man's parts so closely, never had the inclination nor the opportunity to examine the magic wand whispered about at court.

The sight of it stilled her breath within her windpipe. Long, thick and veiny, its size and girth made her groin muscles tighten involuntarily. Hot cream dribbled from her vagina. A cold autumn breeze swirled around them, tossing their hair and garments, but Salena welcomed the cooling sensation upon her burning, perspiring flesh. Her eyes devoured the rod jutting up from the sac nestled before the crisp pale golden curls of his groin. Rubbing her hands up and down her thighs, she flicked her gaze between that aroused cock she now knew could bring her wicked pleasure, and the blazing green eyes narrowed behind the slits of the mask.

Oh...Lord. That *fit inside me?*

"Oh, yes, you sheathed it like a sword's casing. Go ahead, love. Touch it."

Her eyes widened. *Touch it?*

"Yes. And as I've already said, you may speak and move at will now—unless we happen upon anyone. Though we lost them long ago, if we should encounter anyone at all, you will not speak to them or move your body in an attempt to escape."

She shrugged off his command, her mind focused on another matter. "I can really touch it?"

He nodded slowly, almost ominously. Reaching for her hand, he took it and wrapped it around his shaft. Falcon's eyes went limpid behind the mask and he drew in a tight puff of air. His cock felt smooth and silky-soft against her palm, and it was so enormous, her fingers couldn't quite encircle its circumference. He covered the back of her hand with his palm and squeezed, showing her the correct amount of pressure to apply.

"That's it, up and down, tight." He stroked himself using her hand. From the base where his scrotum sat, all the way up and over the tip, she explored the length of him, the very tool that had robbed her of her morals. She quickly caught on to the tempo, so he removed his firm guidance and gripped her hips instead.

She licked her lips, fondling him, inhaling sharp spurts of cold air. White clouds of condensation puffed from both of their mouths. His hands bit into her pelvis as he held her straddled upon his lap. Tiny droplets of white cream emerged from the slit making her wonder what it might taste like. All the while, the horse walked and rocked her back and forth over Falcon's legs.

"I want to fuck you now, princess," he said tightly.

"Now?"

"Now."

She felt something quicken inside her, a rush of wanton urgency. The naughtiness of her position with her legs spread over him, the forbidden exposure of both of their private parts…it made her long to growl and attack as a predator of the forest might.

"But…but here? Outdoors?"

"Here," he confirmed, dragging her close so that her rear scraped over the horse's spine. "Here while we ride."

While we ride? Oh, but the possibility of it, the wild danger, unleashed some hidden beast inside her. Her clit and labia pulsated with desperate, demanding desire. In beat to that pulsation, her heart thumped against her breastbone. White, sticky juices poured from her vagina. There would be no discreet masturbation, no stopping to seek the privacy of shelter. He would penetrate her *now*!

The base of his cock came into contact with her sensitive quim. His hands slid up into her armpits and he lifted her just enough so that her mound was positioned over the moist head.

But the move suddenly sent the fear of King Henry through her. She stiffened. "No!"

"'Tis all right, Salena." He said it soothingly, as if he'd fully expected her sudden trepidation. "I know you are tender there. I will go slow. I will be gentle with you. That I promise."

She had her hands planted on his thick, beefy shoulders. Looking down into his upturned, masked expression, visions filled her mind of his handsome, wounded face poised above her as he pummeled her hole. The gentle passion he'd shown her had been etched in her memory forever. Her first betrothal, Thane's fumbling attempt at premarital lovemaking, his untimely death and her second betrothal to the duke were erased from her past at that very moment. Now, the deep timbre of Falcon's voice caressed her, easing away the memories and the slight fear of being penetrated by that large shaft in a place that even now remained sore.

"I...I'll admit, I ache for it. I-I just fear it will pain me overly much in this shocking, forceful...position."

He ground his teeth together in restraint. "'Tis your choice, then, love." And he nuzzled his face into her breasts. Her nipples flamed with aching need. As he rooted for a taut pebble, he adeptly moved her hips and dragged her cunt over the tip of his cock. She moaned out her pleasure, craving its length within her once again.

"Yes...please..." Her words trailed off when he pushed aside the neckline of her gown with his teeth and exposed one nipple. He sucked it into his hot, wet mouth, his tongue flickering over it so that she cried out. An inferno raced through her so fiercely, she clutched his head to her breast. Unable to resist, she wiggled and twisted until she had the head of his shaft at her entry.

"Slow, gentle...please," she panted.

His arms came around her, holding her protectively against him as the horse beneath them walked lazily through the forest. Falcon released the areola so that he could look up into her face. As he slowly lowered her down onto his rigid cock, he slid his tongue up her chest, along the side of her neck. Gooseflesh of desire rippled out across her arms. Tender at first, her passage tightened against the invasion. But as he gradually entered her, the silky texture of his rod dragged over her clitoris. A slow burn of damp ecstasy erupted in her core. She felt herself go wetter, she coated him with the elixir he could effortlessly draw from her cunt.

Down she went, her passage stretching, taking all of him in, inch by thick inch. Her system jumped with excitement when she felt the tip of him touch a sensitive spot deep inside her. It made waves of bliss ripple out to her fingers and toes.

"Ah…" Her legs came around him and clamped at his buttocks. She clung to his neck, starving for a taste of him. So she took. Salena stole the very breath from him. He opened his mouth and took her in, just as she had taken him into her depths. He groaned into her mouth, his tongue dancing silk-wet around hers. He tasted of the tart wine they'd sipped on as they'd traveled earlier in the morning. She drank of him, now intoxicated by his flavor and the sword he had buried into her core.

"Make me feel it again—please." Desperate now for release, she didn't care that she begged a thief for his prized sword or a scoundrel for his talented touch. She just wanted to attain that delicious sensation. There was no other way to describe it. No way to point out that she would regret it as soon as she got what she craved. Just as thirst could drive one to drink of obviously tainted water, she had no choice but to fulfill a maddening drive within her.

He rocked his hips, his arms tightening around her waist. The gait of the horse beneath them further jarred his movements. It made her scream out her pleasure, and in response, Falcon slammed her down upon his erection so that she was completely impaled by him. They cried out in unison. That secret spot deep inside her became stimulated once again. The weight of her body swallowing him up, combined with the jerky movements of the stallion's pace and Falcon's thrusts, all served to lift her effortlessly to the gates of heaven. Stars erupted behind her closed lids. A flutter and whoosh of wet-hot pleasure barreled through her system. She moaned in unison with Falcon when the surge overtook her to the point of delicious madness.

"It's—oh! I'm feeling it…*again*," she whimpered.

"Ah, Salena…" He clutched her to his chest. One hand went down to press against her ass so that he could grind her closer to draw out the last wave of his own pleasure. He panted, raining kisses over her mouth, her neck, her tingling breasts. "You don't know what you've started, do you?"

Her eyelids came open slow, almost painfully. Reality catapulted into her stomach with vengeful accuracy. That wicked, irresistible ecstasy ebbed, and in its place came a swift rush of remorse and shame. Though she remained joined to him, the sensation still pleasurable on a lesser level, she suddenly wanted to rip herself from his large manhood and run deep into the woods.

"Started?" she echoed. "No...no." Salena lifted herself from him, almost unseating them both. He steadied her, a wary look in his eyes. "'Tis over, bandit. No more. This can't...oh, God help me. I can't continue with this madness. I demand that you return me to my brother and my home this instant!"

She righted her clothing and managed to twist around so that her back was to him—a necessary move when the mortification at what she'd just done overtook her. The tenderness between her legs served a constant reminder of her harlot's heart, her shattered self-control. Degradation now engulfed her. It became edged by the anger that simmered within her breast. And this ire that rushed through her system seemed more directed at herself than at her captor.

How was it that she'd gone from a coveted innocent—with the exception of the one encounter with Thane—to a weak wanton in such a short time?

His movements yanked her from the self-deprecating thoughts. He adjusted his garments and drew her back against his chest. The heat of his body felt so in contrast to the cold winds that whipped around them. She could feel the thud of his heart against her shoulder. It further irritated her that her own heart beat in much the same impassioned rhythm. And she wondered yet another shameful thought...how could one's body be in such extreme moral opposition to one's mind?

Magic. It had to be the domination he wielded with his black magic! There had to be more to this than just a woman suddenly drowning in temptation.

"Sorry to say, but returning you to your kin won't be happening. At least not until I can investigate further and find out for sure who threatens your life."

She cackled hollowly. "Oh, such chivalry from a brigand such as yourself, Robin Hood. Kidnap a lady of the king's court, steal from her home, take unfair advantage of her and then claim to be protecting her." She added a snort of contempt.

"*Unfair advantage*? Think what you like, my —"

An echo in the forest behind them cut Falcon's words short. "Sheldon! I've seen her," the deep voice roared. "She rides with the bandit, Robin Hood!"

"Sheldon!" She'd intended it to be a shout, but her voice came out in a mere whisper. The spell. She'd forgotten the sorcery in which she was forbidden to speak to or alert others. It remained upon her voice — as did the spell upon her body preventing her from fleeing. Her limbs refused to move when she ordered them to jump from the steed and run toward her brother's search party.

Falcon spun Warrior around so that Salena caught a glimpse of her brother through the dense foliage. His eyes blazed with fury, his fiery hair blew about his stone-cold face. She longed to run to him, to sob into his chest as he comforted her. She wanted nothing more than to go home, to collapse in her chamber and forget this brigand who had turned her world upside down. And…she wanted to marry the duke…didn't she?

There was no time to ponder that sudden thought. Sheldon's men raced forward, their warhorses leaping over fallen trees, their swords swiping at dangling limbs. And she heard the bloodcurdling war cry of her angry brother just before the mayhem began.

* * * * *

They'd seemed to come out of nowhere. Falcon could only contribute his carelessness to the deadly charms of this woman. She'd bewitched him from that first glimpse at the tournament, and it only seemed to have gotten worse each time his gaze settled upon her beauty. Now he found himself surrounded by the enemy, a first in his entire existence.

"You will rot in hell, brigand!" Sheldon's massive white stallion charged forward. He held his sword aimed, poised to kill. And there was no mistaking the gleam of murder in his eyes.

Falcon drew his weapon. The screech of metal scraping against metal echoed through the forest. "Get behind me," he barked to Salena.

Salena's body moved into obedience, though he knew by her jerky movements that she fought to defy the spell. Agile for one encumbered by a mass of skirts, she twisted, clinging to him as she moved. With his free arm, he assisted her with adept speed, and sighed when he felt her pressed safely against his back.

"Unfortunately, sir," Falcon shouted. "I'm allowed into neither hell nor heaven."

"Charge, men!" And a flurry of pounding hooves sounded.

Falcon braced himself, quickly noting the positions of all six riders, each now drawing their swords. He whirled Warrior around so that Salena's back faced a gap in the circle of attackers. Drawing firm on the reins, he forced his horse to backward-trot so that they entered a small clearing. Those on the outer edges spun their steeds about and charged the other direction so that they flanked Sheldon and now made a wall before Falcon rather than a circle surrounding him.

"Ah, you think you're so very clever," Sheldon snarled. But the wary hesitation in his gaze didn't go unnoticed. "Onward!" he ordered his men, suddenly halting his beast's steps to allow his men to take to the front line ahead of him.

The first adversary came at Falcon with careless, suicidal speed. His weapon made contact with the attacker, naught but a commoner made to do his master's deadly bidding. He thought to bury his sword within the man's unprotected guts, but instead, Falcon drew Warrior to the side and unseated the serf with one blow by the hilt of his sword. The man tumbled off his horse, falling senseless but alive to a soft bed of leaves.

Falcon heard Salena's sharp gasp, but there wasn't time to address her protest. The second and third riders were upon him, one on each side. It soon became clear that the meager swords were no match for Falcon's heavy, war-wielding weapon. With a quick slice to the dull blades, first left then right, their swords bent and became dislodged from their weak grips. The impact unseated them in almost perfect unison. Eyes wide with stunned disbelief at their sudden positions upon the damp forest floor, they both scrambled up and took off into the woods.

"Cowards!" Sheldon roared. To the remaining two, he growled, "After them or you both die."

At that, Salena gasped again. But Falcon wasn't sure if the surprise was a result of Sheldon's coldhearted words or the fact that the two riders had shot into quick action. More equipped than the others had been, they both drew their bows into position and plucked arrows from their packs. As they drew back, Falcon wrapped his arms behind him, attempting to shield Salena from any stray arrows.

"They hit her, Tremayne, and you die," he said tightly. "That is a promise."

Sheldon made a gesture to halt his men. They paused, the arrows drawn back and aimed square at Falcon's chest.

Sheldon chuckled, an evil, deep rumble. "Well then, hand her over, Robin Hood, and you live."

"Nay."

Sheldon crossed his wrists over the horn of his saddle. He leaned forward nonchalantly, his hellfire-red hair whipping about his bony, pale face. The dark eyes glowed deep and fathomless like a viper's pit. "Nay, he says?" His nostrils flared. "Kill him."

The riders repositioned their longbows and aimed the sharpened arrows at Falcon. It was then he noticed the tall, giant-like figure peeping around the trunk of a massive oak tree.

Ah, Little John. Falcon's gaze riveted to the opposite side of the tree to see yet another of his cohorts. Beauregard Fitzhugh, his familiar lithe frame leaning against the trunk, drew back on his longbow. The sound of Beau's arrow whistling across the clearing distracted one of the attackers. He glanced up just in time to watch the iron tip slam into his shoulder, dislodging his own weapon. Before he could even clutch himself or scream in response, Little John's arrow pierced the other man's upper arm. The bow went clamoring to the ground while both men cried out in agony.

Sheldon glanced about, struggling to see where the stray arrows had come from. "Get down from your mounts, you fools, and retrieve your weapons!"

"Fuck you," the one with the bleeding shoulder hissed out. "Get it yourself."

"You dare to defy me?" he said through clenched teeth. Sheldon sidled his horse up to the man and raised his hand. "Why, I'll—"

The next arrow hit dead center through Sheldon's raised hand. His screech of pain carried over the moan of the wind. Falcon heard Salena's wince and knew without looking that tears poured over her high cheekbones.

"Take what's left of your men and be gone, Tremayne," Falcon warned. "And take with you the comforting thought that my Merry Men are *always* accurate with their intended targets."

Sweat beaded over Sheldon's high forehead. He broke off the arrow and yanked the wooden length from his hand with a grunt. Blood spewed forth, dribbling over the white hide of his horse.

"You'll pay for this, Robin Hood. With your life."

"If only my immortal life were that fragile..." Falcon mumbled to himself.

"Speak up, thief!" Sheldon roared, his horse prancing beneath his trembling body.

"I said, be gone with you — you and all your casualties. And I suggest you all tend to those wounds before fever sets in."

Little John and Beau sauntered forward, fresh arrows aimed square at Sheldon.

Sheldon eyed them, his breath coming in ragged gasps as he held his bleeding hand. His gaze moved to scan his injured excuse for an army. "So," he said to his men, "we ride now…but we'll soon be bringing reinforcements. And the lowly bandit will pay for his mistakes, for kidnapping Lady Salena and harming us all. That I promise with my life."

The unconscious one on the ground began to stir. He looked about, wincing when he touched the knot on his head and drew his hand back to find sticky blood upon his fingertips. "Master?"

"Get up! We ride. Locate your mount and return to the inn." With that, he spun his horse around and sailed through the woods. The two who still remained seated, followed leaving the small man alone on the ground. When they disappeared into the thick foliage, the serf dragged himself up from the wet earth.

"Y-you're…Robin Hood?" the man squeaked. His mousy-brown hair matched his dull brown eyes. The sallow face was one riddled with either illness or fear — Falcon wasn't sure which. He was dressed in the rags of a less-than-valued servant. And his bony frame spoke of one too many missed meals.

"Aye, the Prince of Thieves." Little John spoke before Falcon could reply. As he walked across the clearing, his massive, muscle-packed body moved with all the grace and agility of a man of Beau's thinner stature. John's midnight-black hair swung in long strands around his wide shoulders. "And you're mighty lucky his good, kind heart chose to spare your life and leave you with naught but an annoying lump upon your head."

At the compliment, Salena stiffened behind him, a squeal attempting to erupt from her throat.

Little John turned toward Falcon and stalked to Warrior's side. He looked up, his misty-blue eyes trained upon Salena. "It seems the beautiful lady disagrees with my description of you, Robin, eh?"

Falcon smiled tightly. "Why, I suppose I will let the lady tell you herself." He turned and snared her damning eyes with his own. "You may speak now, Lady Salena. And, as usual, you've permission to move your body as long as you don't attempt escape."

"*Good*?" she screeched, her gaze snapping down to lash out at John. "Kindhearted?" Her unladylike snort accompanied tears. "Well, Mr. Whoever-the-hell-you-are-giant, I beg to differ. Try brute. Try thief of the king's coffers. Try amorous, conceited rogue, for the love of almighty God!"

"And for the lady," Falcon mumbled, "try thorny rosebud."

Beau and John both roared their agreement.

"Who are these men?" Her voice held an edge of fear with that of haughtiness.

"Ah, forgive my terrible manners. Beau, Little John, meet Lady Salena Tremayne, future Duchess of Oxford. Lady Salena, may I present Beauregard Fitzhugh, my highly trusted scout, and John Lawton—or Little John as he's known in these parts—my occasional bodyguard and...brother."

Her stare moved with contempt from Beau's boyish, pretty face to John's manly, handsome features that never failed to stop a lady's heart—and now was no exception, it seemed.

"Brother?" she hissed out, her lip curled in derision. "Ha! You're as different as night and day...with the exception of your thieving talents, apparently."

Little John removed his woodsman's hat and bowed graciously. "Madam. Pleased to make your breathtaking acquaintance." He straightened and set his hat back upon his head, taming the fluttering of his long, billowing hair. Already, Falcon knew what was going through his friend's mind. And though it sent a stab of jealousy raging through his system, he could feel his cock harden at the thought of what would come, as it always did with the two of them.

Salena made no indication of his overt charms affecting her. She narrowed her eyes and speared Falcon with the sharp emotion within them. "Please tell me these men will not be riding with us, Montague."

"Hmm." Falcon stroked his whiskered jaw. "I'm not too sure. Beau? John? Are you returning to camp or are you riding out on another skirmish?"

"I'd planned to venture into London to visit my ma," Beau said as he secured the bow across his back. "John and I just happened upon one another shortly before we heard the shouts."

John slung his longbow over his shoulder and crossed his thick arms over his chest. "And I was in pursuit of you, Robin — er, um, Falcon. It seems you've been delayed by a good night or so."

Falcon flicked a look at Salena. The tears were now dried on her cheeks. She sent him a scathing look, but did not reply.

"Well, the wench is the reason for my delay." As Falcon spoke, Warrior bent his head and began to chew on a lone patch of soggy, dead grass. A chilly breeze rustled his mane, carrying with it the aroma of the early morning rain mixed with soil...and her enticing scent.

"During the planned raid of her manor, I became witness to a murder plot...which included the lady here as the target."

John chuckled. "So you thought to rescue her from her dire demise."

"Precisely."

"You're all fools if you believe such bloody lies from this thief!" Salena snarled.

Beau merely drew out a hunk of dried venison from his codpiece, tore off a strip for himself and offered the remainder to Falcon. He accepted, passing a portion to Salena. She stared at the food in her palm, seeming as dumfounded as if the spell remained upon her voice. But her eyes rose when John stepped up to Warrior so that his chest pressed against her right leg. He spoke with a calm note, though anger simmered in the depths of his sparkling eyes.

"My brother does not lie, nor is he a common thief, milady. I'd advise you to heed my words and remember them well."

"Brother, ha! I see you lie as well, giant. You're no more brothers than myself and this unfortunate serf here."

John's gaze never left her. "Kinship goes beyond blood, Lady Salena."

"Oh? How so?"

"You see, as brothers, we share everything. From the food offered now within your palm, to the fruits of our labors...to our women."

Chapter Six

We share everything…

John's words echoed in her head. Though Salena knew herself to be relatively innocent, that ominous meaning did not pass without comprehension. Her heart leaped into a gallop. She could feel Falcon's warmth against her breasts, but John's pale blue gaze now raked her from head to toe, making her blood boil with sudden lust.

What was wrong with her? Had Falcon cast a spell of carnality upon her, turning her from pure maiden to wanton harlot? The thought of it both angered and thrilled her. How it could be so, she did not know.

But she would not give into this madness!

"I am no one's woman," she ground out, raising her chin to emphasize her words.

John trailed a hand down her leg. Its size made her think of a bear's paw, so very large and lethal. Sparks of reluctant heat ignited wherever he touched. With an inward groan, she tightened her groin muscles as a gush of hot wetness escaped her passage.

"You are Falcon Montague's woman, that I concede."

"Enough, John," Falcon growled. And he reined Warrior out of John's reach.

One of John's inky eyebrows shot up like the tip of an arrow. "Hmm, Falcon, this is quite out of the norm and very…interesting."

"We do not have time to play games. We must ride for camp. Are you or aren't you returning with us?"

"Aye, I'll be returning, though I've no mount—as usual. I came by foot and will meet up with you later."

"Take the serf with you." His voice came out in a half-bark. "His roan has wondered deep within the forest. Retrieve it as you make your way back to our encampment. Once you settle in, see that he is fed and clothed well. And please, if we should be...delayed, brief Lorcan and forewarn him that I ride with the lady."

Not seeming the least bit put out or rejected, John smiled his agreement and pulled the now befuddled serf along behind him. "I understand those types of...delays, my friend. Go forth and have a safe journey."

"That we will. And once you've accomplished settling the serf in and meeting with Lorcan, we shall see you at our...secret locale."

"Secret locale?" Salena couldn't help but question such a cryptic phrase.

"You shall see..." Falcon mumbled. To John, he added, "Farewell, brother."

And John simply nodded to that, shooting Salena one last smoldering gaze before slipping into the foliage. He and the serf disappeared as a spirit might into thin air. With his departure Salena had been left with the memory of his heated touch upon her thigh. And a host of confusion and conflicting emotions.

* * * * *

Salena's conflicting, swirling thoughts of John came to Falcon in a rush among his own curiously territorial emotions. With great self-discipline and a measure of self-disgust, he got on with the matters at hand.

"Beau, please give my regards to your sweet ma." Falcon reached into his codpiece and withdrew a silver coin. "And give her this token of my appreciation for her son's loyalty."

Beau grinned, still chomping on the meat as he caught the coin in his free hand. "Many thanks, my noble man. I will see you in a day or two."

"Godspeed." Falcon waved as Beau gave a lighthearted skip and disappeared into the woods.

"Noble?" Salena neither offered nor needed further words to express her meaning.

Falcon urged Warrior into a trot. "Apparently, 'tis in the eye of the beholder."

"Apparently." She remained behind him and he felt the tightening of her grip as they traveled on. Some sort of odd, fuzzy warmth embraced his heart. He could sense her exciting aura in all manners, sweet scent, soft raspy voice and a sort of unusually thrumming energy surrounding her.

"And what of this Little John character? He seems to think you to be noble, as well, yet I detect a trace of disrespect."

"Disrespect?"

"Aye, in that he seemed to attempt to seduce me—before your very eyes, no less—and offered that ridiculous excuse about sharing."

"'Tis no excuse." He rounded a bend on the path and saw the border of the large meadow ahead, which edged their destination at its nearest point.

"I beg your pardon."

"John and I go way back...centuries."

"Centuries?"

"Aye, princess. I'm sure you now accept my...powers as fact."

He slowed Warrior's gait when the forest opened up into an enormous field. The rolling meadow stretched for miles, the grass and wild weeds still clinging to their green coloring of the season past. Above, the sky remained gray, foreshadowing of weather to come. The scent of winter hovered about, and Falcon wondered what sort of precipitation was in the near forecast. He inhaled the sharp cold air, suddenly eager for snow.

"You ride with a man trapped in immortality—as is Little John. Thus the reason our legend is surrounded by such contradictions as to when and if we ever existed."

"I ride with a liar." She quickly switched subjects. "So he is truly your brother?"

"Nay, not by your understanding of brother, as Sheldon is yours. John is my soul-brother, so to speak. We've been through much together...shared much."

"Yes, shared your women, as he insisted. Well, hear this, my hoodlum prince. I am not your woman to share, and I do not wish to bed down with more than one man at a time. Make that *any* man. In fact, until you burst into my life, I'd bedded no one but that one unfortunate mistake with a former betrothed, who is now deceased."

"That I am perfectly aware of." Her little used barrier had been undeniably tight. The thought of it sent a charge of aching need to his loins. Warrior tossed his head, and Falcon was grateful for the distraction. A white puff of condensation billowed from the beast's nostrils. Falcon's gaze spied a flake of snow ahead, then another, and it pleased him to see the birth of the season he so loved.

"Damn you, I do not wish to be taken advantage of anymore, either by you or your supposed brother."

He pulled on the reins and brought the horse to a halt. Turning, he looked into the depths of her eyes, the blue of them startling above the rosy cheeks. Snowflakes fell, coming to rest on the spiked dark lashes. As he studied her, her chest rose and fell beneath the cloak and her exhalations came out in white puffs of excitement. The picture she made took the very life from his immortal soul. His heart pounded, his palms dampened. And his cock reared up with the need to burrow into her hot pussy and never withdraw.

"Do not wish it? Have you forgotten I can read your mind, Salena? I heard your thoughts, felt the primal lust that coursed through your system when John touched you. Deny it all you want in verbal words, but the truth cannot get past me."

She gasped. "You bastard."

"Nay, just an honest thief." He hadn't meant for that last word to come out with a twist of sarcasm. But damn it, would she ever see him as the man he truly was?

"Please," she said softly, swallowing audibly. "Return me to my brother. You've gotten what you came for, my family's coffers and...my—you've finally bedded me. Have you no decency left?"

"I will not return you to your home until I'm assured your life is no longer in danger."

Salena scoffed, one lone tear glistening in the corner of her eye. "And my life is not in danger in *your* company?"

"Whether you'll admit it to yourself or not, you know you are safe with me."

"Not from your advances—nor will I be from your friend. I'd rather die than bear the shame of this...this situation!"

"Do not fret over John. You are mine. It is our way in that I found you first. But by our soul's affinity, we must share with one another at least once for energy—if the other wishes. And John, no doubt, wishes to have you. And you desire to have him, as well. It is fact. It burns in your very soul. Even now," he rasped, reaching a hand down to cup her apex, "you throb with the thought of being made love to by John and me at the same time."

Her eyelids fluttered shut then open. She stifled a moan. "At the same time?"

"Aye, a common practice, though as an innocent, you would not know of this yet."

"I've..." She drew in a sharp breath when he slid a hand up her skirt and found her wetness. Ah, she was so very ripe and ready!

Her eyebrows furrowed as she fought the lust that he knew slammed through her veins. "N-no. It cannot be. Yes, I concede I've heard it whispered among the ladies at court. B-but I always thought it to be a tale. It *must* be a lie!"

"No, 'tisn't a fable nor a lie. 'Tis a practice that can double your pleasure, *that* I promise you." And he sank one finger into her cunt. Her folds gripped tight and wet around his digit, and it made him yearn to taste her there, to show her more delights of the flesh.

She threw her head back and clamped a hand around his wrist, stilling his movements. "Do not do this to me...please."

The look of conviction in her eyes, despite the rims of passion he saw there, made him rein in his sexual drive. He withdrew the finger and turned, urging Warrior into a gallop. Restraint seemed to choke him by the very throat. His moist finger along with its musky scent mocked him as he stroked the leather strap. How he'd love to throw her upon the snow-spattered ground, toss up her skirts and ram his hard cock into her damp hole. But it would just have to wait. With the incident with Sheldon Tremayne not even an hour behind them, they needed to move on toward camp. They must journey quicker than they'd been before that skirmish, or else face a much larger and better-equipped army. Not until they reached the spring near camp would he even think about stopping again.

Yes, perhaps, he suddenly thought, they would put miles between themselves and Sheldon and have time for that little reprieve with John near the end of their journey...

"There is nothing you can say, no tears you can cry, Lady Salena, that will make me believe you are not curious and do not desire two men at once."

"I do not want to talk about this anymore. Do you hear me, Montague? *Do you hear me*?"

"Aye, dove, I hear you loud and clear, both verbally *and* within the lovely depths of your curious mind. For now, we will set the subject aside...until later."

So he silenced all those words he'd wished to convey to her. Instead, he allowed visions to fill his head. He imagined John sinking himself between her thighs and her subsequent cries of ecstasy. Falcon's balls swelled at the thought of her taking his own cock between those plump peach lips as John pummeled her. He could almost feel the moistness of her mouth, the softness of her skin. And he could hear her moans, sense the rising tides of her release.

Ah, all he could think of was doubling her pleasure, giving her a taste of the dark side well before she'd even dabbled in the straight stuff.

Patience, Falcon. Despite her resistance, she's all yours. And there's plenty of time to show her all the wicked delights of the flesh.

* * * * *

They rode across the meadow for what seemed hours. It stretched endlessly, but now she could see the edge of a new forest up ahead. She focused on her surroundings, struggling to erase from her mind the images his words could so easily sketch there. And she tried helplessly to empty her mind so that he could not read her thoughts.

But it was no use. Even now as they neared the thick foliage, pictures of Falcon making love to her flashed in her mind. Her heart raced, her pussy dampened as time after time, John too entered her thoughts, his large hands stroking her breasts as Falcon buried his rod within her. The mere thought of adding another man, doubling her pleasure, seemed to take her life force from her lungs. Her passage throbbed of its own accord while her nipples remained hard and tingly. Tantalizing flavors burst in her mouth...flavors she hadn't yet tasted.

"How much longer must I endure this forced journey?"

"We're but a quarter-hour's ride away. Soon, you will meet my sevenscore yeomen whom history has dubbed my 'Merry Men'."

"And why have you taken last eve to raid my manor alone? Why were those loyal 'Merry Men' of yours not with you, supporting you as they should?"

He shrugged. "As a rule, we divide up into groups or even singles. It can be more…productive that way."

"I see," she sneered. "Spread the thieving about the countryside for further profit. And fool the king's authorities in the process by giving them one too many crimes at once to investigate."

"Your understanding of the regimentation of such a covert plan makes me wonder if I do not have a valuable recruit within my company."

She did not reply to his mockery but instead scanned the woods as they neared. Towering firs speared upward against the cloud-darkened sky. Elms, oaks and maples mixed with the spruce forming a conglomerated, beautiful, welcoming forest. But its beauty would become her prison. Knowing so, she made note of every path, every unusual tree marking, every babbling brook.

Her thoughts turned to Sheldon's servant from Wyngate Hall whom Falcon had ordered taken to their camp. Mayhap if she could find him among Falcon's men, the two of them could devise an escape plan in secret? The idea brightened the despair in her heart. Hope grew from a mere seedling into a blooming flower. It gave her the fortitude to sharpen her intuition and listen to every word her captor said. So for now, she dashed the thoughts from her mind so he could not detect them.

"You will also meet Lorcan at camp." His tone rang boastful as he maneuvered his mount around a rather wide and deep gorge. Snow continued to fall, coming down in thicker, denser flakes. A good inch or so now covered the ground. Salena shivered from the cold…from the anticipation and dread of what awaited her at his camp.

"He is my mentor. My assigned wizard throughout many centuries."

"Wizard?"

He nodded. "If you think my powers are a bit unconventional, wait until you see Lorcan's. He possesses so much more energy — " Falcon chuckled, " — he ofttimes knows not what to do with it."

Her interest was piqued to say the least. As she tightened her arms around his narrow waist, she caught the rugged scent of him. It stirred something deep within her core, but she forced it from her thoughts and concentrated on his words. This talk of another sorcerer within his camp might prove to be a challenge during her future escape.

"Are all of your men supposed immortals?"

"Nay, of my party, only myself, John and Lorcan have been cursed with life everlasting."

"Cursed? I would think living forever should be viewed as a blessing."

"Nay. Definitely not. One must be immortal to know the curses of it. To live and yet watch those you've grown to care for die time after time…" He shook his head with vigor. "Nay."

Those he cares for? She wondered if this hardened criminal had the heart and capacity in that wide chest of his to love. Being such a ridiculous thought, she let it pass and asked, "So the mortals you recruit to support your causes all die off?"

"Mm, as time passes, so do the lives of those mortals who walk with me. Therefore, we replenish our band of 'outlaws' as needed. You see, we must maintain our historic reputations." She caught the manner of bitterness in his voice. Something about it hummed beneath the surface with sadness and tugged at her heartstrings. But again, she forced the unwanted emotions deep into the recesses of her mind and continued to pick the brain of her enemy as she hugged him close.

"Why is it, Falcon Montague, that you tell me all your secrets?"

Stillness echoed loud and clear around them. But for the crunch of the steed's hooves upon snow, silence reigned. The smells of leather and man wafted up to entice her senses. Though the air could chill one to the bone, Salena reluctantly took in the warmth of his body, leaning closer to seek the potent energy of him. She pressed her torso to the wall of his back and turned her cheek, resting it upon his straight spine. Finally, he spoke, his voice low with an ominous ring.

"I do not know."

She allowed him another moment of reflection before further unleashing her curiosity. "I wonder…are you, in a sense, their magical king, their strongest commander?"

"According to Lorcan's prophesies I have been 'the chosen one', the one to lead in many causes, the one to fight for those less fortunate. And nay. My powers do not match those of the old man Lorcan's, for he is the almighty wizardmaster. But my talents slightly outweigh those of my brother."

"John…"

"John."

"And what cause," she asked as the dense woods opened into a large clearing, "do you fight for now, this day?"

"Hmm, well, to begin with, the king's Pilgrimage of Grace rages on as we speak, my sheltered lady. The commoners have forged forth with an uprising that I wholly support."

"Ah, yes," she agreed. "The grudge against the king for the negative influence his man, Thomas Cromwell, seems to be having upon him. As well as protests against the government's eradication of papal supremacy and confiscation of certain properties. Pure rubbish."

"It seems you're not as sheltered as I'd first thought," he said in a cheery yet cryptic tone. "And rubbish, you say? You must realize that with the northern counties beginning to come under martial law, many people are being hanged on mere suspicion of hostility against their landlords and the king. My cause is for that lowly man, the man who fights against hardship, the tenants who are caught up in unrest and the threat of eviction by their landlords — who have the iron-fist backing of your king."

"You speak untruths."

"Nay, my pretty lady. I speak life as your serfs and servants' kin know it. For selfish profit, the king is allowing expulsion of these hard-working tenants, either illegally or for the slightest default. He is turning a blind eye to the famine and death, the turmoil and sheer suffering put upon these people by their land masters. Why are they being put upon, you hopefully ask? So that their landlords may take over the land in order to enclose large areas for their own gain. To convert the land they once shared with these people into fenced sheep pastures for enormous profits."

"No…"

"Yes. And there's no need for you to deny it. I'm well aware your rich estate is one of the top producers for the king. And your brother is the epitome of the ruthless master I speak of."

No! I don't believe a word of it. But I will humor him, try and see his twisted side of things for a bit of self-entertainment.

Falcon grunted in derision, apparently in response to her direct thought.

"So you tell yourself these torrid tales in order to justify your thieving and mayhem. Do I have that correct, at least?"

He stiffened the slightest bit within her arms. "As the saying has gone for centuries, I steal from the rich and gift the poor. In this case, I'm giving back to the poor — in a roundabout way — what is already theirs and has been stolen from them without good cause."

She couldn't help but let out a boisterous, tinkling laugh. "Oh, yes. How could I have forgotten? The self-righteous vigilante, the infamous Robin Hood."

He didn't take time to rebut or agree. Instead, he guided the stallion through the first clearing and into another. Its splendor was such that it stunned her to speechlessness and dissipated all thoughts of uprisings and turmoil from her mind. An enormous rock nestled into a steep hillside. Thick foliage of spruce and undergrowth surrounded a small pool of water at its base. Her gaze fell to the surface of the water. Steam curled upward in plumes of inviting heat. She sighed, instantly aware of what it was that she spied.

"A hot spring."

"Ah, yes, but 'tis more thought of as heaven."

Salena swung her gaze to Falcon's handsome face as he glanced over his shoulder and soaked her with a mysterious stare. It was all she needed to make an educated guess.

"So this is the 'secret locale' you mentioned to John."

"Aye."

At his simple confirmation and the deep note to his voice, her heart leapt into a gallop. "He is not here."

"No, he takes care of business. But we are here and we will be taking full advantage of Mother Nature's amenities before riding into camp."

"Meaning?"

"Meaning…we bathe." And he dismounted, leading the horse to a flat boulder that jutted out over another making a roof of sorts. "Come." And he raised his arms to her.

"W-what do you mean, exactly?"

He sighed and grasped her waist, dragging her down from the steed. Falcon looked down into her face, his eyes making her shiver more than the snow now falling in torrents of flakes. She could hear a faint bubbling of water in the pool below them. Steam looped up and over, enveloping her in a misty warmth. The palms of his hands branded her, even through the thickness of the cloak.

His breath warmed her cheek as he spoke. "I mean just what I said. We bathe. Now. Together—you and I in this heavenly pool of water. You will love it. It is refreshing and cleansing all at once."

Her mouth fell open. "No…I refuse to bathe with you! And I do not wish to become overly chilled and risk illness."

He rolled his eyes upward toward the overhanging rock. "I vow to keep you safe from illness…and very warm. If I tell you it may be your last chance to cleanse that lovely body of yours, you will still refuse me?"

"Last chance?"

"Though I can read some people's minds periodically and cast spells of things such as physical obedience, I cannot tell the future. That is Lorcan's forte, at times. Therefore, I advise you to bathe while you can, pretty lady, else you be left with the possibility of ne'er another chance for a long time to come."

Periodically, he'd said. So, he could not *always* read her mind or that of others. Well, that was a small comfort within the fog of this nightmare.

"Oh, yes, I've forgotten. The savage will no doubt be thrusting his primitive ways upon me during my captivity. Which, no doubt, will include not providing decent bathing facilities."

He grinned, and something about those gleaming white teeth made her heart twist and her hormones race. "Nay, milady. *This* is my decent bathing facility. Though it is a few minutes ride from camp, it is just uncertain how often we will be afforded a chance to return. Being the stealthy brigands that we are, at any moment, we may have to uproot and take flight."

She warred with the possibility of never being given a chance to bathe again for an indefinite time period. Though uncommon this day and age, daily cleansing was her normal ritual, and she loathed the prospect of being denied that usual luxury.

"Put in such a way, I concede. But I will bathe *alone*."

He winked through the slits of the mask. "You will disrobe quickly. Quickly because, though your brother has long ago lost our trail, we still must be cautious. Once you disrobe, enter the pool. I will follow and we shall have a most enticing dip in the hot spring."

His words served to combust that spot between her thighs. She panted as she spoke. Though voluntary, her body moved into obedience mode, disrobing as ordered, beginning first with her cape, then the gown.

"Please not...t-together. You cannot bathe *with* me...not n-naked and out in the open." A sudden whoosh of cold air assaulted her skin. Her bare feet froze against the snow-covered rock and her nipples hardened to the brittleness of icicles. Behind her, she could feel the soothing heat from the pool upon her backside. The stark contrasts drew her irresistibly to seek comfort.

"Isn't naked the manner in which one usually bathes? But I'm no fool, love. I would warm my body and cleanse it, too, now that I've the opportunity. You know we've not the time to take turns at it, and besides, I will do what it takes to sample your delicious charms..."

His words echoed in her head as she removed her nightrail. Biting cold air nipped at her flesh and she trembled, hugging her nakedness against his burning gaze and the chilly wind and snow. Her clitoris throbbed with a scorching heat, and she thought no spring water could be hotter than her own blood at this moment. This man...he seemed to be turning her to mush with or without his hocus-pocus.

He took her clothing and placed the garments over Warrior's back. Hastily, Falcon disrobed and stood before her, both of them nude and shivering in the cold and snow. Captivated by what she saw, her stare moved down over his body, over the wide shoulders and chest, the taut dark nipples, the rippled rib cage and flat abdomen. She licked her lips, suddenly longing to run her tongue from his now unsmiling mouth down to his navel. Salena's gaze fell upon his manhood and her pulse leapt into a sprint. The magnificent tool jutted in half-hard arousal from a nest of dark blond curls. Below it, the swollen balls seemed to cradle its base. Powerful, corded legs were positioned apart, dappled by pale hair.

She raked her fingernails over her thighs, longing to test the texture of every single hair on that brawny body of his. How she hungered to rip that mask from his face and run her fingers through the long, straight mane billowing out from beneath his feathered woodmen's hat. She imagined she'd then run her nails down through the light smattering of hair across his chest. Next, she'd explore the softness of the light fur covering those strong legs. And lastly…she yearned to delve into that thick base of curls surrounding his cock, to grip that massive organ in her hand.

The mere thought of his cock held captive in her palm made her sweat and start to go to him. But instead, the hot spring called to her, offering another tantalizing choice. Now fully undressed, she turned and set one foot onto a rocky step several inches below the water's surface.

"Ah!" She groaned when the heat enveloped her frozen foot. She could swear she heard a sizzle as she set her other foot onto the step. The pleasant sensation of thawing flesh drew her deeper into the waters. Steam plumed upward surrounding her calves. She took the underwater, rocky stairs one at time. The heat swallowed up her knees, then her thighs. Her nipples hardened to painful nubs. She could feel the throbbing in her pussy, and just as the heat rose over her labia, hot stickiness oozed from her pussy. Behind her, she heard the water slosh and Falcon's sigh of ecstasy as he entered the pool. The thought of his naked body so close to hers sent a wicked shiver through her blood.

She continued to walk deeper into the spring groaning out loud when the hot liquid embraced her chilled skin. The level had just reached her shoulders when she felt his arms go around her from behind. He dragged her back so that her buttocks pressed against his granite-hard shaft. Her pulse leapt in her throat. Almost simultaneously, his warm lips were there at her neck stilling the thump of that erratic pulse. Gooseflesh shimmered out over her shoulders, down her torso and legs, out over her arms and fingers.

"Oh, Salena…you are so irresistible, so very gorgeous." He reached around and cupped her breasts with tender care. Lazily, he rolled her nipples between his thumb and forefinger. Shatters of desire burst out and downward turning into a slow trickle of flowing need between her legs. Languid bliss washed through her. Her body felt weightless cradled within the hot wetness of the pool and in the circle of his arms. Unable to help herself, she allowed her head to drop back against his shoulder. Above her, snowflakes fluttered down cold and quiet. But beneath the surface of this heaven he'd brought her to, it seemed lava churned around her, the eye of that volcano stationed directly behind her.

"I…I think…that you are irresistible, as well."

One hand shot up to cup her jaw. He turned her face so that she had to strain her head around to look into his smoldering eyes. "If you continue to say things like that, milady, I cannot be held responsible for my actions."

His mouth came down on hers in a warm loving swoop. He held her face in place, his other hand kneading at one breast. A heavy ache bloomed there, soaking down into her womb. She tasted passion edged with a dangerous yearning that was, indeed, irresistible. His long tongue explored her eager mouth, sucking the desire from her. It didn't take long for him to move on to new territory. He released her bosom and she felt the long stroke of his palm moving lower. The trek wavered from side to side, as if he couldn't decide what part of her body he wished to conquer. Her belly fluttered with anticipation when the pressure slid down her right rib cage, across her navel to her left hip.

He dragged one fingertip from her pelvic bone diagonally to the mound of her curls. The swirl of that digit around her clitoris caused her mouth to tear from his.

"Oh, God." Panting, Salena struggled to keep her eyes open. Focusing on the snowflakes, she watched as they fell upon the water's surface and instantly dissolved into the heat. Just like her body seemed to be melting into his. The hand that had been holding her jaw captive swooped down and gripped her chest. With a firm grasp on the swell of one breast, he slammed her flush against his arousal. Falcon ground her ass into his hard cock and flickered his finger over her nub simultaneously.

When he sank two fingers into her passage, she didn't even notice the tenderness his earlier lovemaking had left behind. How could she perceive pain when pleasure seemed to envelop her in such a delicious carnal fog? Salena didn't know where her own hot juices ended and the steaming water began. He pumped her like he had with his cock only hours ago.

No longer could she keep her feet on the pool's bottom surface. Her legs floated up and it seemed to be Falcon's cue to make a change. He yanked his fingers from inside her and swirled her around in the water to face him.

"Put your arms around my neck and your legs around my waist and hold on real tight, darling."

She obeyed, nearly sighing when the tip of his shaft speared her hole. Salena throbbed with the urgent need to be fully penetrated. His chest pressed warm and unyielding against hers. His hands did wondrous kneading things to her rear making her shiver and perspire all at once. Bloody hell, this man tempted her beyond reason!

"Falcon...I...I need it again."

"Ah, Salena." His eyes glittered like emeralds through the holes in the mask, as if the gems were cradled in rich black velvet. His breath came out in anxious puffs of white, so like she imagined a dragon's might in those folklores she'd heard. "I fear there is no turning back. At my first taste of your charms, I was utterly smitten. I warn you, you will not be getting free of me anytime soon."

It was said with such conviction, such emotion, that it nearly brought tears to her eyes — nearly. It wouldn't do to succumb and surrender her heart to his dangerous wizardry. Instead, she pushed through the steam and slammed her mouth into his, drinking in the sweet flavor of him. Not seconds later, with his mouth still sealed to hers, he lifted her hips and drove her down upon his cock. She moaned and took him all in, her ankles locking just above his buttocks. Caught up in his expert rhythm, she could have sworn she heard a groan from somewhere afar. But she couldn't open her eyes. All she wanted was to wrap herself around him, to be completely consumed by Falcon Montague and the soothing waters that surrounded them.

The corded muscles in his arms tightened around her waist as he lifted her up and down, stroking himself with her tight wetness. Brief spurts of cold air battered her skin cooling the unbearable heat of her passion each time her wet flesh broke the surface. Hot curls of ecstasy simmered deep within her cunt and she could almost feel it again, the bliss that he could so easily gift her with.

Salena inhaled catching the scent of snow and cedar upon the breeze. Once again, she heard the moan from afar. Almost to the brink of sweet insanity, she slowly opened her eyes and glanced over Falcon's shoulder.

And there he was.

John...standing on the boulder near Warrior with his codpiece shoved down below his sac and his shaft in his hand. Snow fell upon him, but he seemed not to notice, seemed transfixed by what he saw in the steam-topped carnal waters below. The sight of him made her gasp with both discomfiture and stunned pleasure. Her pussy spasmed, soaking Falcon's cock with a new gush of honey. John was an enormous man with an enormous organ—there was no mistaking it now. The name of *Little* just did not fit him, especially not at this aroused moment, she thought.

Unable to help herself, she allowed her gaze to rake over him, even as Falcon continued to bounce her upon his penis. John's body emitted utter animal power. He stood with his legs planted apart, his braies taut over muscular thighs. From the distance, his hair appeared almost blue-black in the gray light of the storm as it fluttered over brawny shoulders. The unusual color and texture of his hair made her think of the descriptions she'd heard about those supposed "savages" across the ocean in the New World. The very thought of this wild "native" even so much as laying eyes upon her naked body made her groan with naughty eagerness. He wore a feathered woodman's cap much like Falcon's, but it did not hide the shoulder-length hair. And since he wore no mask, the blue intensity of his pale eyes against the bronze skin had the power to soak her with both his cold indifference and hot passion.

To watch and be watched while in such an intimate position...it brought to the surface a beastly, feral side of herself she did not know existed. As if addicted to some courtly, delectable concoction, her gaze drank of him while her body drowned in Falcon's talented touch.

"You will love it when he finally joins us, angel." He traced the curve of her neck with his tongue. Little sparks of hot exploding stars rained over her flesh and fanned the flames he'd already ignited. "Four big hands instead of two—" he found her asshole under the water and outlined its tightness, " —a score of fingers instead of ten, two cocks—" he drove deeper into her, " —instead of just one."

She gulped a cold burst of air into her scorching lungs. Release loomed ever nearer. Her entire pelvic area throbbed with a heavy ache that was both maddening and delicious. "How...how did you know he was there?"

"You mean do my powers include eyes in the back of my head?" He chuckled and sank that single long finger into her rear. She cried out, shocked by the fiery delight that such a forbidden taboo could provide her. It moved her closer to impending release. Panting, she loosened her muscles and let his finger all the way in, frantic now to be filled everywhere.

Unable to resist the sight of John performing that primitive act while Falcon drove her to new heights, Salena's eyes moved back to the bank where he stood. Bombarded by so many overwhelming pleasures at once, her vision blurred and the orgasm reached out and stroked her for a brief moment. It receded when Falcon removed the finger.

"No," he went on. And he teased the outside of her hole again making her groin muscles tighten with need. "I sensed your changes and read your wanton thoughts, felt you get wetter and more desperate in your quest for that much-needed gratification. And since I already expected him…"

He turned in the water so that their profiles faced John. Salena's first reaction was to shrink from sight, to protect her bare breasts from the pair of rabid gazes that devoured her. But she was simply too far gone. Temptation won out.

"I—I can't do this. You can't…oh, *God!*" The orgasm gripped her at the exact moment she saw the thick white fluid squirt from the tip of John's cock. His eyes remained on her as they rode together on a hot, steamy wave of bliss. Falcon's release came only seconds following her guttural moan. It seemed the three of them sang a song in unison, a song of complete and expressive pleasure.

Her eyelids closed shut allowing the last crest to wash through her. She shivered trying to force the regret away so that it would not taint what had just occurred. Falcon gripped her with desperation, raining kisses over her mouth, her nose and cheeks, her neck and shoulders. She sighed pulling him closer so she could lay her head upon his shoulder. As she did so, she gradually opened her eyes to allow herself one more look at John before slipping back into the bitterness of her reality.

But he was gone. "Where…where did he go?" She heard the disappointment in her voice and prayed it hadn't sounded as pathetic to Falcon.

He didn't even glance up. His hands lazily massaged her back and rear. Holding her tight, he said, "Back to camp, of course."

Relief flooded her stomach. She didn't wish to face him so soon. Even if a ride into their encampment took another partial hour, it would be minutes she would not have to face the man.

"So fast? After...?"

Falcon let out a low rumble of delight. "Recall he's also immortal. John possesses powers of invisible movement. He can disappear at the blink of an eye and travel at incomprehensible speeds in that form. No doubt, he is already back with the others."

Lifting her from his shaft, he kissed her mouth, pressing his soft lips against hers time and time again. It warmed her heart, despite the cold of realism setting in. Pulling away, she shrieked, "Invisible? Why, you must be crazy. That's simply ridiculous!"

"In the same manner my mind-control powers are ridiculous? Nay, princess," he said blandly as he walked toward the stairs with her still wrapped about him. "'Tis naught but truths I speak."

She dropped her forehead to his shoulder as he stepped up onto the first stair. "I must be in a strange dream. I'm still lying in my bed, I'm still lying in my bed, I'm still—"

"To repeat it will not make it so. 'Tis no dream, Salena."

And to prove the bitter reality of it, he climbed the rocky steps and carried her from the water. Icy winds assaulted her warmed flesh. The wet ends of her long hair plastered to her back and froze. She inhaled a lungful of protest. "Oh...oh, it's so c-cold."

But she soon found out he wouldn't make her suffer much longer. His hands went up and swirled through the falling snow. A funnel of warm air wound around each of them. Salena savored the sensation of drying flesh and hair, and the warmth of her clothes suddenly tucked around her.

Falcon grinned wolfishly, now dry and fully clothed, as well. "Another little talent I possess."

She glanced down at her cloak and back up at him. "And why didn't you just do that the first time?"

"The first time?"

"Aye, thief." Her blood was starting to boil, only this time it had nothing to do with his hot magic hands. "Last eve when my garments were soaked. You took me to the stable room at the inn to get them dry."

"Ah." He spanned his large hands around her waist and lifted her up onto Warrior's back. "You must be referring to when your clothing became soaked due to your lame attempt at escape."

"Oh!" How was it that he had such a flair for getting her dander up only a minute after pleasuring her? She glared down at him. "That is because your fight against me is unfair, *master*."

"Unfair?" He mounted behind her this time. Warmth enveloped her as he encircled her with his arms and took the reins in one hand. The other hand nestled against her rib cage beneath her breasts. Something about that gesture made her feel safe and secure...secure with a bandit, of all things. The thought of it further fueled her ire and confusion.

He spun the horse about and took out across the edge of the clearing. Soon, they detoured onto a forest path. "How so is it unfair?"

"It does not take a brilliant scholar to understand it, Montague," she threw over her shoulder as they galloped along. "Your sorcery is unfair. Without it, you would have lost and I would have escaped you long ago. You and I both know it."

He merely grunted his disagreement.

"You did not answer my question. The one regarding why you did not just fling your magical hands about and dry me and my garments the first time."

"Simple, my love. Because I needed a good excuse to strip your cumbersome skirts from you. And because due to the type of immortal I am, my soul must release through sexual delights in order to strengthen the very powers I've used over you."

They entered a denser area of woods. She could detect the scent of burning logs. "So if you were to be deprived of fornication for a long period, you would be powerless?"

"Aye."

"And if you do what...John was doing?"

"Self-pleasure? Masturbation?"

She nodded, mortified by the blatant terms. Salena could have sworn the roots of her hair ignited with the heat of embarrassment.

"No. I must have the real thing. Pussy, woman, even oral stimulation by a woman works," he said hotly into her ear. At his brazen words, shivers shimmied down over her flesh, but she made no indication of his influence over her. "I must push my cock into the wet folds — or mouth — of a female and release my semen in order to replenish my strength."

Or mouth? His words conjured up all sorts of wicked images. It brought a hot rush of stickiness to her core. "So if I can somehow deny you, your hocus-pocus dies out?"

"You are not the only woman in the world, Salena, with a mouth and a tight cunt and pearly-white, slick juices."

She stiffened. Perplexed now at her own emotions, she wondered why the thought of him with another woman increasingly seemed to irritate her as the day passed. "Ah, another woman like Molly? Or just like you've tried to offer me to another man?"

The sounds of idle conversation gradually escalated as they drew nearer to camp. The delicious aroma of roast pig drifted on the air. Salena's stomach growled in anticipation of food to fill that empty space in her abdomen. Up ahead, she could see dozens of men dressed in much the same manner as Falcon. They lingered around a massive fire where a pig had been strung over the flames.

Falcon tightened his arm around her, pressing her back against the tight wall of his chest. In a low growl, he said, "I will never give you up to another man. Never. You are mine for as long as I want to have you. John will but sample you as decreed our brotherhood. And one trio session is all that is required to give us both a massive dose of long-lasting powers…for a time, anyway. When it is done, you may choose to deny him forever, if that is your wish."

"Having one woman together in a trio is nothing more than a selfish way of strengthening your black magic?" Her voice came out shrill and indignant.

"That and the sheer pleasure of it, of course."

"Ha!" She tossed her head back, the hood of her cloak falling across her shoulders. "Then you *both* can just go and find some other woman who's willing to give you what I refuse to."

"Falcon!" The voice sounded like an angel's. From the crowd of several score of men emerged a figure dressed just like all the other outlaws. Only this figure possessed the soft curves of a woman. She leapt into a sprint and approached the horse, her feet coming to a halt when her eyes finally rested upon Salena's face.

Salena had never regretted her words more than she did at this moment. Stunned, she looked down into the most beautiful, striking features she'd ever seen. Jealousy burned in her abdomen. A sudden need to take back her saucy suggestion of using another woman plagued her.

Her gaze swept the woman from the tall, shapely form clad in men's clothing to the long pair of golden-blonde braids resting upon massive breasts. Salena knew her first-ever sudden yearning to slap a woman's face.

And in her gut, she knew this to be Falcon's woman.

Chapter Seven

Falcon looked down into Grizella Kenrick's gorgeous face. Somewhat self-destructively, he allowed the guilt to spear him arrow-tip sharp. Why hadn't he thought of her before now? Ever since he'd snatched Salena from her chambers, he'd not given Grizella another consideration. Not even to stop and think that he may be subjecting Salena to this hellcat's wrath by bringing her here — or subjecting Grizella to emotional pain.

Though looking now upon Salena's snarling profile, he wondered if Grizella would be in for the fight of her life instead.

The woman had never been a true love interest of either Falcon or John. Grizella was one of their fiercest warriors and he'd always admired her courage and tenacity. True, he and John had had their power-energizing romps with her, especially on long raids in which they'd go for weeks without other female contact. Grizella knew the score. She gladly gave of her talents and then some without so much as a single complaint or demand. There were no ties, no pairing off or sharing space as a committed man and woman might. The three of them always went about their business uniting only when libidos demanded it. Theirs was an understanding of minimal necessity...at least that's what he'd thought. Grizella had never before now made any territorial claims on either Falcon or John.

He twisted his mouth into a wry grin. *Well, I suppose she's had no reason to complain until now, until spying this lovely, gracious creature in my arms.*

"Hello, Griz." He dismounted and drew Salena down. The two women never took their narrowed eyes from one another. Though he'd normally have laughed it off, he knew this situation did not merit humor, at least not for the time being.

"Falcon." She said it tight and formal, her amber eyes glittering like a cat nonverbally making her territory known. "You're late. I'd begun to worry over your welfare."

"Well, I had a bit of a delay."

Grizella crossed her arms under her ample bosom. "I see that," she said through clenched teeth, one booted foot tapping in the snow.

"Who is this woman?" Salena suddenly asked, whirling toward him. Would it be wrong, Falcon wondered, to glorify in the sharp tone of jealousy he heard in her voice?

He sighed. "Lady Salena Tremayne, meet Grizella Kenrick, my...most trusted warrior."

"*Pleased* to make your acquaintance, lady." Grizella thrust out a calloused hand daring Salena to take it.

She accepted the offered hand and shook it with female gentleness, her mouth compressed into a firm line. "Likewise, Miss Kenrick." She nodded, the ever-regal princess. Her composure did something to Falcon's innards, twisting them with a vile combination of admiration and disappointment at the fact that she did not spit back.

Finally, Griz swung her gaze up to snare him with her suppressed fury. "Shall I find her a place to bed down for the night, Falcon? Eh?"

He winced. His stomach twisted in knots. "Well—"

John suddenly materialized at Grizella's left. "Falcon must guard her, Grizella. We have a...situation going on in which she must be protected at every moment of the night and day."

Ah, thank the gods for John's quick thinking!

Grizella whipped her head around and snared John with a mind-your-own-business look. "Who asked you, giant?"

Now that he had his bearings a bit more straight, Falcon spoke with the assurance of a leader. "Griz, he speaks the truth. And you will cease with the sass and show John respect."

She blinked, her stare moving over all three of them, one at a time. The last victim was Falcon. "You're sleeping with her, aren't you?"

Salena gasped. Her hand shot up to slap Grizella but Falcon caught her wrist just in time. "Enough! Out of both of you."

His charged spell-gaze moved to Grizella who stood with her hand on the hilt of her hunting knife. "You will go now, Grizella, with John and prepare for the coming raid."

Falcon glanced at Salena's surprised expression when, by the command of his spell, Griz turned toward John, a glitter of anger simmering in her eyes. John put his arm across her shoulders and, together, they both disappeared into thin air.

Salena blinked at the illusion, but Falcon was too wary to elaborate for her benefit. With her face turned toward him now, he snared her with his controlling stare. "You will go with Gowain there—" he jutted his chin toward the young man who sprang into action, "—and he will show you my place of rest. And you will not ever attempt to lay a hand on that woman again."

Salena's gaze narrowed and he thought at this moment she more resembled that spitting cat than Grizella had. "I loathe you," she snarled under her breath as her body moved into action. He watched as she trailed off following Gowain, his gaze lingering on the vague sway of hip beneath fabric.

"Ah, well, it seems you've captured the maiden's heart. And she yours."

Falcon spun to see Lorcan sitting upon a low oak limb that jutted out parallel to the ground. Snow fell around him in a shower of white flakes yet it seemed not to touch him. He wore the usual black monk's robe and his long silver hair and beard stood out stark against it. Around his neck he wore the usual *Centaurus* medallion. Its large blue, cat's-eye-shaped stone glowed even by the dull light of the waning day, the silver chain dangling long to his breastbone.

Falcon had been told it was the medallion that would one day be passed down to him.

"Your jesting normally tickles my heart, old man. But alas, I see no humor in my dire situation."

Lorcan stabbed his crystal staff into the snow and leapt from the limb. The wizard, Falcon thought, was so much more agile than his feeble body appeared.

"Eh, 'tis not a situation, son. 'Tis fate."

Falcon strode to a fallen tree trunk and sat. He spoke while studying the busy activities of his many loyal men as they prepared for nightfall. Some set up watch in designated trees, others formed snug beds into the recesses of the cliff they'd claimed as a protective wall. Others still, fashioned tents by arranging blankets over tree limbs close to the toasty fire. The hog was nearly done roasting and would feed his Merry Men upon waking with voracious appetites and a hunger to raid.

"Please, Lorcan," he said on a sigh. "Do not go babbling in your usual cryptic fashion. Come right out with it, for I am weary due to this unusual journey I've experienced in days past."

Lorcan perched beside Falcon and gripped the staff with gnarled hands. "Your lady. You must know I've seen into the future, I've seen her as your intended. And though Grizella is not yet aware of it, it has been her role in this fate to force Lady Salena to see her heart more clearly where you are concerned."

It didn't surprise Falcon in the least. From the first moment he'd laid eyes on Salena, he'd felt a connection to her. In the back of his mind, he'd yearned to arrive here, longing for such words from this prophetic seer. There existed an undeniable bond between him and Salena that far surpassed all he'd experienced with anyone since coming into being eons ago. Now he knew it had been more than her beauty that had drawn him to her, more than her sensual charms.

Yet things did not add up.

"But she is mortal."

Lorcan nodded and turned, puffs of white pluming from his nose and mouth. Falcon never failed to be startled by those eyes…all white. Save for the lone black pupils in the centers, they contained not one speck of color within them. He began to hum in that ancient Gaelic tune. "Mortal, aye. And I warn you…there is much unrest and possible danger ahead!" Lorcan suddenly groaned. "'Tis all in how you handle it…"

Falcon set his hand upon the quivering leg, thin and bony even through the thickness of the woolen robe. The gesture always calmed Lorcan in these rare outbursts, but he seemed not to notice this time. Instead, he rose and jutted the staff toward the dark snow clouds, the other hand fisted. Lorcan tipped his face upward and energy swirled above him. With the movement, snow came down harder as the winds whipped up and fluttered his garment.

"Oh, gods of Fate, hear my plea. Lover and vigilante, set him free!"

Falcon stood and stepped toward him, suddenly fearing for the old man's existence. He'd never seen him quite this agitated before. "Lorcan, what—"

But the winds died down almost as quickly as they'd whipped up. The snowfall slowed and began to fall more gentle and serene, fluttering to the ground weightlessly.

"You shall find the way," Lorcan roared as he stroked the medallion. He nodded vigorously and gradually lowered his head so that Falcon could peer into his mysterious eyes once again. And he could have sworn he saw tears glistening in the white orbs.

"Wizard, please, what ails you?"

"You shall find the way, I say."

"What? To become mortal myself and finally die with this woman I may grow to love? Ah, if only…" Falcon pushed up from the seat and paced before the fire. "But if I must endure the pain again—such as with Marion—of watching her die of old age after possibly loving her for decades…nay, then I'd prefer not to love at all. Lorcan, do you hear me? You cannot allow me to love if—"

He turned then, cutting himself off. The old sorcerer was gone and in his place a cloud of lavender smoke whirled and gradually dissipated. As usual, when he'd completed his performance and had his say, there was, in Lorcan's view, nothing more to say.

But Falcon had plenty more questions. Though he knew Lorcan would continue to speak in puzzling riddles. It was just, as always, up to Falcon to figure it out.

* * * * *

"You may rest in here," Gowain said, gesturing to the low-ceilinged space. They were both hunched, though Gowain far more than Salena. His tall, lanky frame had towered over her out-of-doors, yet now, they both stooped, their eyes level by necessity.

She glanced around and took in the hard rock floor, and the small fire that crackled in the center, a curl of smoke wafting up through a hole in the cave's ceiling. Looking up through the gap, she could see the darkening sky beyond the overhang of firs. Every so often, a stray flake of snow would waft down and make the flames crackle and spit. Along with the burning wood, the scent of pine needles filled her nostrils. Off against one low wall, she could see where the aroma originated. A bed had been prepared with the needles, a bear's pelt thrown over the thick pile for comfort.

John. She instantly knew it must have been he who'd readied Falcon's resting area. Salena shuddered, attempting to tamp down the excitement that suddenly hurdled through her body. Had he also had himself in mind to share this brigand's lair?

No, Salena, you mustn't think such depraved thoughts.

But she couldn't separate those thoughts from what lay before her. The space warmed her chilled bones…just as the hot spring pool had.

"Here," Gowain said with a boyish grin, crouch-stepping to the opposite wall, "is the private corner, or you may refer to it as the chamber pot."

Here eyes located another hole, this time in the floor of the cave. "That?" From above, a small stream trickled down the wall and through the hole's opening. "But I…"

"The water will carry the…waste down and out, away from camp."

"Amazing." She'd never heard of such a thing!

"Aye," he said, his hazel eyes alight as he made his way to the cave's narrow exit. "One of nature's true wonders. Either that or…Falcon's magical doing."

"Please, do not remind me."

He chuckled, straightening as he made his way outside. Gowain turned back and lowered his head, peering in at her. "Begging your pardon, milady, but…"

She arched a brow. "Yes?"

"When the spell is not upon you, I feel it my duty to advise you for your safety to stay right where you are. Unless Falcon gives you permission otherwise, that is."

"Gowain, with all due respect, I truly appreciate your concern. But know this. Unless your master's black magic you so proudly speak of is used, I take orders from no one. I do as I bloody well please. Therefore, I advise *you* to mind your own affairs."

He blinked, clearly startled by her reply. "Then, with all due respect in return, Lady Tremayne, I must warn you, you will be watched with the sharp eye of a hawk. That would be, rather, well over sevenscore hawks' eyes, by the way."

Falcon came into view then. She would recognize those braies anywhere…and what bulged within them. He hunched down clearing the cave's opening, and slid her a look of victory at his man's support. Despite the taunt, every pulse point in her body palpitated. She could swear her heart burst in her chest. She likened the sight of him after only a few moments of absence — their first separation since he'd abducted her — to a lifetime without water. Salena thirsted for him, in spite of the woman Grizella — nay, *because* of her. Jealousy raged through her system like a poison, driving her to him rather than away.

And beneath all that covetousness, it infuriated her immensely that the unfamiliar emotion even existed in her heart.

"Gowain, I am pleased by your loyalty as always, son. Please, go and check with Little John. He will compensate you well for your hard work and allegiance these past weeks. Your family is in dire need of food as we speak. On the morrow, make the short journey and ease their suffering." He clapped him on the back. "Go now and get some rest in preparation for the night's raid."

Gowain nodded with a beaming smile. He afforded Salena one quick, cautious jerk of the eye before sauntering off whistling a merry tune.

Falcon tossed aside a linen-wrapped bundle and dropped to his knees, his head clearing the low ceiling. He crawled toward her, a predator's gleam in his eyes. She noted that he'd removed the mask and it afforded her a full, dangerous view of his face. She was surprised to see that the slashing injury across his cheek and temple seemed strangely to have disappeared. The wound had lent him the dangerous look of a pirate, but now, without the disfigurement, the handsome look of him made her heart palpitate in her chest. Salena's knees weakened and she felt the slight edges of a swoon coming on. How could she fight such a magnificent rogue as this?

"Must I cut your tongue from that beautiful head of yours?"

"You wouldn't!" She backed away still hunched, and collapsed upon the bed. Soft fur cushioned her fall. The scent of pine needles and man overtook Salena. Excitement overwhelming her, she planted her elbows behind her, a trapped animal's lame attempt at defense.

"Nay," he growled, climbing upon the bearskin. "I've not done such a thing to anyone—yet." He kept advancing on the pelt until she had no choice but to lay back. He hovered above her, the firelight flickering over the planes and angles of his face. His breath warmed her lips, so close were their proximity. Those wolf-like eyes glittered and remained open, never leaving hers. They looked into hers with an intensity that stilled her breath.

It seemed time wavered, as if they were held suspended together in a realm of their own. Somewhere off in the distance, the fire crackled, and the sounds of the camp settling in for the early evening faded away. Her body tingled with unleashed energy, though she could not move a muscle. He'd cast the spell for her to follow Gowain into the cave, but once she'd obeyed that order, her body had become her own. Yet she could not move. The moment became etched profound and indelible upon her brain.

"Make love to me," she suddenly whispered, her own words surprising her. But there was no mistaking the heat that pounded between her thighs. She could swear scalding-hot wax dribbled from her pussy. All it seemed to take, she finally accepted, was one smoldering look from him and she yearned for his erect cock to plunge into her depths. She did not know how it had happened in such a short time, but…she'd become addicted to her captor.

He blinked in surprise at her request. "Ah, the lady has gotten a taste or two of the delights of the flesh. But is she aware the best is yet to come?"

Yes, she suspected there would be more to his carnal web of surprises. She pressed a hand to his cheek. "Where—how did your wound mend so quickly?"

He took her hand and kissed the palm causing flutters of heat to race to her breasts. "'Tis John's doing. He has the power within his touch to change, to alter, to heal."

"This John…he is turning out to be quite the mysterious man."

Falcon forced a look of envy into his eyes yet he smiled confidently. "You pine for another, milady?"

"No, he merely fascinates me on a different level. As for this bandit who has abducted me and brought me to his den of desire?" she purred, tracing his lip with her fingertip. "I finally admit...I do pine for *him*."

He didn't offer any reply. He merely looked at her with an indefinable emotion glazing his eyes. It made her long to reach for him, so she did. Gone was the need to suppress her silent longings. Why bother? He could sense her desires and read her thoughts anyway? And she no longer wished to deny herself another moment.

She slid her arms around his neck and drew him down, opening her legs to accommodate his hips. His half-hard shaft pressed into her wetness. Even through all the layers of clothing, the move was potent and it made her growl deep in her throat. His dark magic seemed to diffuse over her, into her, right into her throbbing passage. But it wasn't enough.

"Take me, please. Despite the fact that I can loathe you at times, I also yearn for your...arrow to spear me, to bring me to that swift pinnacle."

"Salena..." It was all he needed to say. His mouth swooped down and claimed her lips. He must have sampled some wine since ordering her to go with Gowain, for he tasted of ambrosia. She hungered for more, her arms tightening around his neck and taut shoulders. Salena closed her eyes giving herself over to the thrill of wickedness. Her legs circled his hips, but he immediately untangled them before she could hook her ankles together.

He tore his mouth from hers. "Nay, little filly, I need your legs free for this..."

Her eyes fluttered open. Salena let out painful, short spurts of air. "For what, warlock? What black sorcery will you wield upon me this time? Aye, I am your prisoner, I now concede to that truth. But please do not make me beg for your charms."

Falcon traced her trembling lower lip with his finger. His gaze followed its path down over her jaw, her neck and collarbone, her heaving breasts. She could have sworn fire tipped his finger. A blaze ignited wherever he touched. Her hair stood on end, her heart beat erratically, her nipples tightened against the fabric of her gown.

"You shall never have to beg me to do what my soul has hungered for since I laid eyes upon you at court. Now relax. Allow me to introduce some new charms to you." And he smiled down at her, his expression tender yet wayward.

She obeyed, though it was of her own free will. He moved lower, his finger tracing the outside of her garment. He pressed firm across her rib cage, spanned his hands over her waist.

"Close your eyes and loosen every muscle in your body."

She inhaled and complied. It really was quite liberating, she discovered, to lie back and allow him to worship her. The touch of those large hands slid down over her pelvis, lower to her thighs and calves. He reached her boots and one by one, he removed them. Falcon took one bare foot in his palm and rubbed it between his hands. Blood pumped through her circulation warming everywhere he massaged. Salena sighed, the bliss of it sending a ripple of gooseflesh up her leg, over her torso to her scalp.

When the soft and wet sensation of lips fluttered over her arch, she had to rein in the urge to yank her foot from his grasp. At first it did nothing but tickle. However, when he stuck his tongue out and dragged it from her heel to the ball of her foot, she nearly came off the bed with the surprising pleasure of it. Before she had time to acclimate herself to the shivering desire the move had produced, he drew her second toe into his mouth.

"Oh! Oh, Falcon. Oh—"

Her words were cut short when he bent her knee as he swirled his tongue around the toe. Reaching up her thigh, he pushed aside her garments until he found her core. He made one circle around her clitoris before burying a trio of fingers inside her. She couldn't help but groan aloud. Her moans echoed against the stone walls. He pumped her, plunging into the sticky mess between her mons lips. All the while, his tongue twirled and sucked, moving on to the next toe as the one before became desensitized.

Ecstasy raced through her veins. She slapped her hands onto the pelt and fisted them into the long fur. "Falcon...Falcon I'm going to—"

Just as she arched her back to welcome the orgasm, he retreated.

"No...oh please, do not stop." She reached down between her legs, grappling for his hand. He pulled it out of reach.

"Salena, I told you to relax. Lie back." His voice held a trace of barely contained restraint. It told her she wasn't the only one in desperate need and the realization gave her a sort of wild satisfaction.

She did as he bade. "You are a cruel master, but still, I want you."

Falcon took her leg and stretched it out, setting her ankle upon his shoulder. "Then you shall have me. Or should I say, I shall have you?"

The cryptic words passed without comprehension until she saw his intent. He bit and licked, sucked and scratched first the flesh of her calf, then her inner thighs, then...

"W-what...are you—" His mouth closed over her pussy. Salena screamed her pleasure, heedless of her voice carrying out into the woods. Falcon's tongue did wicked, evil things to her. And she wondered in that moment if he were the devil in disguise masquerading as a thief in the dark forests of England.

He swiped her labia and darted his long tongue into her creamy hole. She gasped, her stomach quivering with the intense sensation of it. Instinct took over and she raised one knee, the other leg still slung over his shoulder. Salena thrust her pelvis up against his face so that he fucked her with that talented tongue. His arms went under her ass and hooked over the top of her legs so that he could hold the swollen lips open. He made noises that boiled her blood, noises that indicated bliss and a rabid hunger of his own. Salena thought at that moment she'd lost her mind, but she soon realized there would be more torture to come.

Pinpricks of wet-hot fire blasted through her veins when he removed his tongue from her hole and swirled it around her pebble-hard pearl. Her breath caught, released, caught, released. Fisting handfuls of fur, she bucked upward, her head rolling from side to side. She was almost there. The sensation of it made her groan with anticipation.

Further riding on that instinct, she gripped his head, sinking her fingers into the thickness of his hair. He growled and increased the pressure. But it wasn't enough. Each flicker took her to the gate and back but not through it. Clamping her teeth together on a feral moan, her palms spanned his scalp and she ground his mouth into that magic spot. Her hips moved in short little bucks, making his tongue vibrate hard and fast over her clitoris.

She lifted her head suddenly needing to watch him devour her. Those emerald eyes were already watching her face intently. The glazed look in them told her he experienced maddening paradise just as she did. The sight of him devouring her most private area pushed her upward toward that peak she desperately reached for. She could almost taste what he tasted, could swear she could feel what he felt. The scent of her own arousal wafted up to tease her nostrils. The lapping noises he made sounded against the backdrop of the autumn winds as they whistled outside the cave. It tapped into a beastly urge within her, and she knew in that instant she was lost to this man forever. The intimacy they shared coupled with the ambiance of the setting nearly moved her to tears.

"Falcon…" she whispered on a gasp. "I never knew such… Ah, I love watching you feast on me down there."

He grunted, never removing his mouth from her. His tongue wiggled faster and it brought to mind the flapping wings of a hummingbird. Her eyes struggled to stay open, to watch him satisfy her so expertly. The explosion came upon her with almost deadly force. Her heart stilled. She couldn't breathe. Red-hot bliss crested over her and she growled out her release. But it wasn't the end. As soon as she reached the pinnacle, riding its last few waves, he forced several fingers into her passage and pumped in rhythm with his tongue. The move brought her back to the glory and delight of his carnal heaven.

"I'm going to—oh, yes, again!" His fingers pummeled her, filling her up like his cock had. Her legs wrapped around his head making her skirts slide further up and bunch across her abdomen. She couldn't hold onto his head anymore. The blaze of ecstasy, so close on the last one's heels, forced her to surrender completely. She slapped her hands onto the fur pelt as his tongue and fingers drove her along the path of insanity. It went on forever it seemed.

Salena gasped in and out, turning her head toward the cave opening. Crying out, she finally reached the last ridge of madness at the very second her eyes fell upon John. He sat just inside the cave's narrow opening, outlined by the early evening dusk, his back leaning against the rocky wall. His head turned toward the interior of the cave and firelight danced over his rugged, handsome face. Her gaze fell ever lower. She could see the enormous bulge in his codpiece. He rubbed himself outside the garment while his eyes held hers from across the space. An image of that large cock filled her mind, of him stroking himself, stroking her. Amazingly, she felt desire soak her core once again.

Falcon slowly withdrew his fingers and crawled up and over her. He planted his elbows beside her head and she turned to look up into the restrained face of a beast.

"It is time." He said it huskily, dragging his sticky mouth back and forth over her own. She could taste the salty flavor of her sex on his lips, could detect the wild fragrance. It made her hunger to lick all the white cream from his face. But his words had caused her pulse to pound dangerously fast.

"Time?"

"Time for you to couple with us," John rasped crawling toward them on all fours. "Both of us...at the same time. I...I need your energy."

Chapter Eight

John brought to mind a stealthy wolf, his eyes glittering with hunger. She caught his woodsy scent, like and yet different from Falcon's. Falcon shifted to her right side, propped himself up on his left elbow and played lazily with her breasts. Her nipples puckered beneath the bodice of her gown abrading over the fabric. John moved calculatingly closer, and she could swear a cloud of warmth cocooned her between the two men.

Two men! Excitement knotted in her belly. She recalled Falcon's words… *Four hands, a score of fingers…two cocks.*

What, in heaven's name, will I do with two cocks? And at the same time, no less!

"You will enjoy them just as you've enjoyed two hands, ten fingers and one cock, milady," Falcon replied to her thoughts. "It will be twice the pleasure."

His words made her quake in disbelief. She remembered Falcon's explanation that the two of them must mate with one woman in order to temporarily fuel their immortality. Though the anticipation and curiosity of it held her fascinated, she couldn't help but feel as if she were being used like a harlot.

"Your talents are quite enough for me, Falcon," she countered, yet her voice held a note of indecision. "And I do not wish to be a toy for a pair of rogues, to be tossed aside once well-used."

They both burst out in a deep howl of laughter.

"Rogues we might be," John said with a potent grin and a charming wink. "But a toy you will never be to me. You hold a place of honor in my heart, not only because you will help replenish my already diminishing powers, but because you are my spirit-brother's chosen one."

"Chosen one?" She glanced to her right noting the look of vexation Falcon shot at John.

"Lorcan can better brief you on that particular point."

"Lorcan? The old wizard you spoke of?"

"Aye, that old wizard knows things we do not. He speaks in riddles, his most recent being a bit of a shock. But now isn't the time to discuss such trivialities...is it, John?"

It seemed to be John's cue to go forth with their plan. Propped on his elbows and laying on his stomach at a right angle to her, he lowered his head toward her mouth.

"Wait!" Her hand came into contact with his barrel-thick chest. Hard muscles bunched beneath her palm. Caught off-guard by the pleasantness of touching John with Falcon at her side...it rendered her into a stuttering, incoherent babble. "I...oh, but... Now you can't—I just don't know. Wait! I said no!"

Apparently, he didn't hear her, for John's mouth slammed into hers. At the same moment, Falcon slid his right hand up her thigh making hot blood pool in her womb. The mouth against hers was different yet the same, larger yet precise and just as talented. His tongue slid around hers, hesitated, darted deep into her mouth. It retreated swiping over her lips.

"Ah, I taste your own juices upon your lips. Nectar to a starving man," John growled and claimed her mouth again. Sparks of confusion and need drugged with wanton desire burst from her tongue and shattered down and over her vee.

Falcon rubbed his braies against her hip. "Touch me," he whispered in her ear, and his hand took hers and dragged it down and into his garment. Fully erect, it felt like a silk-covered rod of iron inside her curled hand. She gripped the length of him, marveling at his size.

"Ah, yes, like that," he rasped.

Salena groaned when John softened the kiss, pulling back to make a path down her jaw and neck. The move caused her to tighten her hold on Falcon's shaft. He hissed almost simultaneously with her when John suddenly tore back the neckline of her gown and cupped one breast. Her areola went tingly hard even before his warm mouth closed over it.

Through the fog of lust enveloping her, she groaned out loud when Falcon found her pearl. John's left hand shot down then and found Falcon's hand. He used it as a point of reference and found her pussy hole, sinking one of those long, thick fingers into her as Falcon continued his strumming of her clit.

"Oh, my God. I'm doing this. I'm really doing this!"

She couldn't take it any longer. Salena removed her hand from inside Falcon's braies. She hooked her right arm around his neck, her left around John's. Hungry, simply famished, she dragged both of their mouths to hers. Ah, he'd forgotten to forewarn her of the pleasure of three silky-smooth tongues, three pairs of soft, wet lips. Three chests touching so intimately it made her nipples ache with the need to be devoured.

Falcon must have read her mind because he tore his mouth from theirs and growled, "Sit up. Take that cumbersome garment off."

She obeyed but there was no need for the force of a spell. Eager anticipation had her sitting bolt upright and jerking the gown and undergarments off. The cave felt warm as the fire crackled behind John. The two men came up on their knees and stripped their own clothing off. It simply paralyzed her lungs to see the firelight dance over both wide shoulders, both tight chests, all those rippled abdomen muscles…and the powerful, fully erect shafts.

Two of them! Here gaze bounced to the left then to the right and back again. Her pussy flooded with an outpouring of wetness she could not contain. Salena started to reach out to both cocks. Her heart suddenly thumped as if to warn her she must halt this madness. She drew her hands back and flexed her fingers.

"'Tis all right," John murmured. "You can touch us both at the same time."

"Salena," Falcon said in a low, husky voice as he reached for her hand and wrapped it around his rod. "Do not be afraid. Go ahead. Explore and satisfy that carnal curiosity of yours." He took her other hand, leaned in front of her and curled it around John's cock.

John hissed so sharply she started, thinking she'd hurt him. He slid her a tight smile as if he clung to what tiny remnants of control he had left. "I'm fine…just very excited by your soft touch." His words combined with the pale blue haze of bliss in his eyes sent a new surge to her womb—as did the silk-over-rock feel of the two cocks in her hands.

What should I do now?

"Move your hands at the same time," Falcon offered. "Ah, yes, like that…"

Their heads went back at the same instant and it made her think of two wolves howling to the moon. She stroked them in unison, her hands getting the feel, the rhythm and the pressure down in a matter of minutes.

"Salena…" Falcon gritted out through clenched teeth. She glanced up at him, spellbound by the look of passion in his eyes. "How would you like to kiss them, like I kissed you down there?"

"Kiss them?"

"Aye." John scooted on his knees moving closer so that they touched her outer left thigh. Falcon did the same at her right. She got an up-close perusal of both delectable manhood specimens. They were both veiny and long with little droplets of pearly-white juice oozing from the slits. She knew this meant they neared that blissful point where more semen would shoot from the tips once further stimulated. The mental picture that thought conjured up made her breath come in short, eager spurts. She licked her lips, longing to taste their juices as Falcon had tasted hers.

She brought them closer together above her lap so she could compare and examine them as she continued to fondle them. Their lengths were almost identical, though John's appeared slightly longer, perhaps a half-inch at most. She suddenly saw the irony in his name, "Little" John. There was nothing at all little about this man, and knowing so made her heart race, her feminine ego swell.

Falcon's cock had a bit more girth. She could not span his entire circumference with her hand but she could barely span John's rod. They both jutted proudly from nests of curls, though where Falcon's was golden-blond in color, John's was as black as the hair upon his scalp.

When they each closed a hand over her breasts, her head fell back, the long length of wavy hair swishing sensuously over her naked buttocks. Their talented palms skimmed and sizzled over the soft bulk of her mounds and puckered nipples. Fingers pinched, tweaked and pulled sending a backlash of fire to her already flaming pussy. Ah, it made her hungry, made her feel like the wolves she'd likened them to moments ago.

She lowered her head and inhaled catching a conglomerated manly scent in her nostrils. Her nose moved closer to Falcon. He smelled sweet yet somewhat salty. She turned her head and drew in John's sexual aroma. She detected the same woodsy undertones but a pleasant muskiness all his own filled her lungs. Together, it was a potent combination and it made her clit throb when she turned back to Falcon and pressed a soft kiss to the head of his penis.

"Ah, yes. Since I am your only true man, Salena..." he ground out when she flicked her tongue out to taste the cum. Bitter saltiness burst in her mouth. "I must get the first ever feel of your mouth around me, not John."

The sound of the possessiveness in his voice made her heart race with pride and an unexpected joy. She was starting to understand the dynamics of this strange situation with John. While Falcon had claimed her as his woman, it was her duty to provide him and his soul-brother with the energy needed to strengthen their powers. Yes, there was excitement in John's presence. His rugged handsomeness was very pleasing to the eye, as was the beauty of his powerful body. But there was not that indefinable depth of strange and deep emotions she felt with Falcon. And as some women did their duty by entertaining their husband's guests in their homes, so did she. Only Falcon was not her husband and the type of entertainment she provided far surpassed dinner, the throwing of lavish balls and serving a goblet or two of wine.

This was the way of Falcon Montague, Robin Hood, legendary thief of hearts. She'd had a difficult time accepting the reality of his claims to immortality and powers yet she'd experienced it first hand and could not deny it. How was it that she'd gone from being the inexperienced, intended bride of Edward Devonshire, the Duke of Oxford, to this charismatic scamp, Robin Hood's plaything in two day's time?

Had he simply captured her heart or was it the workings of his black magic?

Suddenly, she didn't care if magic played a role or not. Salena stroked John with her hand and closed her mouth over Falcon's cock. She rejoiced in the growl it elicited from them both. Lust unleashed full force in her system and she let out a growl of her own. It came from deep in her throat as she swirled her tongue around Falcon's huge organ. He hissed and she sucked harder. She tasted his delicious flavor while pleasuring another man with her hand. Her pussy throbbed with anticipation at what would come, and eagerness picked up in an impatient pace in her belly, galloping, rushing forward.

John moved closer so that his cock touched her cheek. "Taste me now."

In a frenzy, she released Falcon with a *pop* and sucked John in. His flavor was saltier, his scent more musky. She gripped the long length of him and relaxed her throat, attempting to take as much of it in as she could. Her right hand pumped up and down on Falcon's shaft, still moist from her wet mouth. Together, the three of them moaned and grunted. But it still wasn't enough to satisfy her anxious needs and ruthless curiosity. She wanted them both in her mouth, had to see what it would be like to double the pleasure she now tasted, felt, smelled.

Two cocks...

Falcon's words echoed in her head prompting her to take action. She removed her mouth from John's rod and rose onto her knees. Salena tugged until the front of their cocks pressed together, the tight sacs bulging in a group of four massive jewels.

Falcon groaned.

John muttered, "Jesus!"

And she took them both in.

"Holy mother—"

"Son of a—"

Her mouth stretching wide, she screamed around the double bulk in her mouth when they reached down simultaneously, Falcon to her frontside, John to her back. Salena feasted on their mixed flavors, struggling to hold still for their talented hands. Falcon's fingers found her swollen pebble. He alternated rubbing it with penetrating her pussy so that she almost saw the edges of release. Sticky juice dripped from her cunt. She could smell her wild arousal even over that of these two irresistible men.

John found her soaking-wet pool, coated his finger and dragged it up to twirl it around her tight asshole. Falcon had already shown her the delights of this forbidden taboo. And since they already had her in a wild frenzy of need, she *had* to have it again.

Removing her mouth from the cocks, she thrust her rear back and screamed "Yes!" when he sank his finger into her ass at the same time Falcon invaded her pussy with two fingers.

"Ah, she is ready," John said huskily.

"Aye, I agree." Falcon shifted, pressing a hand down on the bearskin until he lay on his back. To Salena, he looked up at her and nearly barked, "Straddle me."

The sudden removal of all those digits from her holes gave her a brief moment of disappointment — until she saw Falcon's manhood pressed against his belly, just waiting for her to mount him.

"But what about John and the…"

"You will see, Salena. We will pleasure you at the same time. And it will be a phenomenal experience for you."

She swallowed audibly, swinging her knee over his waist until she was perched over him, his cock barely brushing her cunt. Salena planted her hands on his hard chest looking down into his face, rigid now with painful restraint.

"Yes, there you go." Falcon spread his legs, and she watched with confusion and a sense of excitement when John went behind her and settled between Falcon's thighs.

"But first, I must heal your tender flesh. In such a short time, you've already experienced quite a bit of activity," John rasped in her ear. His hands massaged her shoulders, her spine. Shivers of relaxation combined with sexual tension slammed through her blood. Honey dribbled onto Falcon's cock.

"Heal me? How?" she asked, glancing over her shoulder.

Suddenly, she remembered mention of his healing touch. Her eyes snapped back and grazed over the length of Falcon's forehead and cheek where only hours ago, a deep gash had been. Now, his face was flawless, not a scar upon its beautiful planes and angles. John had repaired that jagged, raw flesh, just as he would make the escalating tenderness between her legs go away.

John's big hands skimmed down over her ass. He cupped each globe, massaging as he went. Taking one cheek of her buttocks, he lifted and separated it from the other. The move made warm air swish over the smeared wetness of her crotch. He caressed and moved ever lower, avoiding her anus until he reached her mons. It made her fall forward onto her hands so that she was poised over Falcon in doggy fashion. Cupping the whole of her womanly flesh, John rubbed hard and long. The strangeness of the sensations that bombarded her made her gasp and she held in a breath. Salena closed her eyes, taking in the ice-cold numbness as he continued to rub her. She sighed as it soothed, doing her best to hold herself up against the relaxation that bathed her.

Falcon stroked up and down her arms, and when she forced her eyelids open, she looked down to see him staring up at her with an affectionate, almost loving expression.

"Hold still, love, and just let it soak in. Soon, it will be warm and cold all at once. But you will no longer be sore and inflamed there. You will be able to take us both in, and John will heal you as needed afterwards."

Take them both in? The phrase alone almost made her come. The images it dredged up in her mind made her pant out her impatience. Her pussy did, indeed, begin to warm while at the same time still remaining cool. The tenderness was now completely gone. And in its place came an urge to be torn into.

"Now." She turned her head back and forth, looking first at Falcon then at John over her shoulder and back again. "Whatever you plan to do to me, please, I beg of you, do it now. I burn for it. I must have you both before I explode!"

John chuckled softly. "Falcon, what a lucky man you are."

"Aye," he agreed, reaching up to hold her face in his hands. He pulled her down for a kiss at the same moment John gently pressed her forward. Holding her hips, John guided her over Falcon so that the tip of Falcon's cock barely speared her tingling mons. She arched her head down and took Falcon's mouth with hers. It was a different kind of kiss, one of long-lived passion and some indefinable fondness. Their tongues mated and she tasted of the remnants of her own cream.

She sighed when John's hands spanned her ass and spread her apart. He reached between her legs and gripped Falcon's hard cock, moving it around in small circles so that the tip became coated by her juices. With his other hand, he reached up and gripped one of her shoulders and pulled down, spearing her onto Falcon's shaft.

Her head came up. "Oh!" she screamed, suddenly filled by him, knowing another man watched the penetration, even participated in the act. She had to still herself to combat the premature orgasm. No, she wanted to draw it out, to make this fantasy last as long as possible. She tried desperately to think of something else, anything but the carnal craze that seized her.

As if that weren't enough mind-blowing stimuli to endure, John spread her ass again. She nearly leapt to the cave's ceiling when she felt the unmistakable, silky wetness of his tongue exploring her anus, darting in and out, swirling around the sensitive hole. It made her groin and ass muscles clench and then relax in spasm-like motions. Her entire body quivered with an agonizing thirst for more, yet she did not think she could take the titillation of it another moment longer.

"Oh, Falcon…" She tried desperately to keep her gaze on his. Perspiration beaded his forehead. His eyes were glazed with rigid restraint. But he couldn't possibly be feeling the depth of lust she was. "I-I can't bear this. It is too…too wicked!"

"You just wait. The best is yet to come, my love." He pulled her down and lifted one of her breasts, closing his mouth over the tight pebble. Sweet heat curled down and met with John's swirling tongue. It slithered around to tease her pussy where Falcon's cock remained motionless but buried to the very hilt.

She never once imagined there could be such fervent mania involved in that overlooked hole of her body. The level of heat rose with the slickness John added there. It made her finally relax and push against the tongue. She hungered for it to spear her deeper, hotter. As if he sensed her need, he slowly slipped a finger into her anus. His tongue continued to play around the stretched flesh emphasizing the extent of the hidden nerves there. Falcon moved, slowly rocking his pelvis up against her. They weren't the long, deep and forceful strokes of usual. He took care, respectful of what went on on the other side. And by his next words, apparently knowledgeable of what would come next.

"Now relax your ass muscles, darling. Do not tighten up," Falcon advised, his voice husky and panting.

Before she could ascertain exactly why he suggested it, the finger slipped from inside her. Disappointment washed through her and along with it the reaches of relief vanished. But the frustration was short-lived. She looked down to see John's large hands planted next to Falcon's elbows where he rested them as he reached up to span her ribs. Heat and smooth, rippled flesh covered her naked back. One hand moved out of view and she stiffened with pleasure when she felt the tip of John's cock touch her anus.

"Relax, Serena," John whispered in her ear. "You're very ready. You've been moistened, your muscles are accepting of the invasion to come."

"Invasion?" she whimpered.

"Blissful invasion," Falcon corrected, and he reached up and hooked a hand around her neck. "Do it, John," he ordered, and slammed her mouth into his.

She almost bit his tongue when John pushed an inch of his shaft into her ass. The first reaction was to indeed tighten up and ward off the invasion.

John stilled his movements, his hot breath ragged in her ear. "Relax, beautiful. I guarantee you will love it. You will have the most intense, lengthy orgasm yet."

Falcon held her mouth against his, rocking his hips up and down so that she could now feel the delicious ache of pre-orgasm reaching out to her. Her clit rubbed hard and rhythmic against his lower abdomen. She inhaled taking in the potent mixed fragrance of pussy juice, male pre-cum, perspiration and the musky faint new scent that came from John's breath after that trio kiss they'd all shared. It made her growl against Falcon's mouth, and she planted her hands down next to his shoulders to gain better leverage.

Concentrating on relaxing her muscles, she tore her mouth from Falcon's and said on a pant, "Yes... Give it to me, John. I-I'm ready. Gently, give it to me gently."

Both men moaned their excitement. She pushed downward, relaxing her anus further. And John entered her, inch by inch, with one long, firm stroke. Salena screamed, utterly astounded by the instant bliss of it.

"Oh. My. God." She rocked against Falcon. He rocked back. John followed suit until the three of them had a mind-shattering rhythm going. In and out they went in sync together. They withdrew in unison causing her to yearn for more. They sank their cocks deep inside her at the same time, filling her so completely she clawed at the bearskin fighting for more.

"Salena..." Falcon whispered, dragging her mouth back to his. She devoured his mouth, longing for that one last hole to be filled.

"Ah, you're so tight," John said through clenched teeth. "I'm—I'm going to come very soon..."

"Mm, mm, mm," was all she could get out. She didn't want to abandon the long tongue that fucked her mouth. Her body was alive and tingled over every inch of her flesh, every layer of her skin. She likened the sensation of having every cavern filled to finally coming home after not realizing she was lost. Flames of lusty fire ignited in every bone, every muscle of her body. She couldn't get enough. She moved frantically, bucking up and down between the two hard bodies, desperate to be filled deeper.

Falcon's hands were all over her, wherever he could find room to caress her. John's lips grazed over the nape of her neck. He suckled there, sending renewed ripples of lava to her pussy and ass. She dwelled in absolute heavenly bliss, couldn't get her legs and rear spread wide enough.

But the sweet frustration finally reached its peak of satisfaction.

"Oh, God, Falcon," she whimpered against his mouth. His eyes opened slow and languid and she would never forget the glazed look of passion there. "I'm about to feel that feeling again, only…"

"It's coming in your ass, too?"

"Yes, it's—oh, ah! *Bloody* hell!" Her moans echoed against the rocky walls. Firelight danced over three twined bodies, but deep blue sparks burst before her vision making the light seem so much colder than what Salena felt. Shortly after the long male groans of release filled her ears, hot stickiness coated her womb and deep inside her anus. The sparks went on and on, centered in her entire pelvic region, bursting through her veins. She clutched Falcon's shoulders drawing out the final flickers of unbelievable lust and pleasure. Hips moved against hips, hands skimmed over limbs clutching soft flesh, hard bodies.

And finally, it was over.

Salena lay spent across Falcon's chest. Perspiration slicked their naked bodies. John held himself up so as not to impose his weight upon her. Gradually, he slipped from inside her and she felt an emptiness coupled with a cool whoosh of air across her damp back. His hand slid down and massaged her tender anus. Again, cool-hot warmth permeated her flesh. She sighed, grateful for the relief, for she knew had he not imparted his healing touch to that area, it might have been very possible she would have been unable to walk on the morrow.

"Thank you, Salena," she heard him whisper.

Gradually, his hand glided up toward her tailbone and away from her ass. She lay there inhaling Falcon's manly scent, soaking in his warmth, listening to his steady heartbeat and slowing respirations. His hands lazily grazed her back. It sent pinpricks of relaxation down her spine, up into her scalp. Drowsy, she listened for John to shift and settle at her side. But all she heard was the crackle of the fire and an occasional murmur from Falcon's band of men outside the cave.

"John?" She lifted her head and glanced over her shoulder just in time to see his body glow with intense energy then flicker into nothingness.

* * * * *

Falcon looked up at the breathtaking sight she made. If he didn't know better, he'd say she'd *tazired* him into stunned speechlessness. What she'd just allowed to happen had been the most phenomenal, power-gathering *intromosis* he'd ever experienced in his entire existence. He felt energized enough to last him an eternity. Immortal forces burst through his body even now, a full minute or two following the *mergent* coupling.

"What troubles you?"

"John, where has he gone?"

"He has returned to his own space. The *intromosis* process is complete for now. Thanks to you," he said, smiling softly at her, "we have both been gifted with energy needed to perform our talents."

"*Intromosis…*" she rolled the word around on her tongue.

He studied her as understanding lit upon her expression. The reaction of his body as he inhaled her rose-tinted scent, combined with all the aromas of a glorified bout of lovemaking, simply stunned him. He wanted her again! His hand rose and he combed his fingers through her long sable tresses. The strands glittered by the light of the fire. She cuddled against his hand and he could swear he heard her purr like a feline. Her bright cat eyes appeared pale and crystal-like in the cave's ambient light.

The analogy made him stiffen in surprise. The eyes…they were exactly the shade and shape of that melded into Lorcan's *Centaurus* medallion.

Dizziness washed through him as he continued to stare at the lovely pools. *You must know I've seen into the future, I've seen her as your intended.* Lorcan's voice echoed in his head. And suspicions reverberated with it.

147

Lorcan help me, but I just might understand a piece of your puzzle. I'm in love with her! And it feels nothing like that with Marion had, nothing like ever before…

The realization made everything come together. This was the first time he'd ever *really* loved someone. She would be his by fate yet he still did not know how to solve the problem of her mortality. *Gods of our right, I cannot take another loss of a loved one!* His immortal heart just could not survive watching this woman die and being forced to move on into eternity without her. He could not watch her die — ever. Tomorrow, decades from now, it did not matter when. It was the one thing he was certain that could kill his immortal supremacy. He would do all in his power to sustain her and to continue to solve Lorcan's riddle of how she could be his intended yet still be mortal.

And he would start with her brother. He raked both hands through her hair, marveling at the long length of the strands as he continued to ponder his next plan. She sighed and collapsed onto his chest. Her soft breasts pressed against his torso and something about the tender moment further sealed his love for her.

It sealed, too, his resolve to make her love him back.

He must return to Wyngate Hall and confiscate that letter. Falcon thought he knew where the key was hidden, thanks to his cunning spy skills the night he'd overheard her murder being plotted. He'd attempted to tap into the thoughts of both men in the room but he had failed. That skill was selective and seemed to be proximal-related as well. But if he could return to the manor's library and locate the letter, it might be enough proof to talk her into staying with him. He wanted her willingly at his side. Sure, he'd gotten her addicted to sex, but he knew by her intermittent thoughts that she still planned and plotted an escape.

Something odd and painful twisted in his gut. She wanted to return so she could marry the duke, that he was aware of.

"Salena." His hands gripped her arms until she rose up to stare into his eyes. His universe tumbled and imploded, for he saw the beauty there marred by wariness.

"I must leave you for the night."

"Aye," she said on a wistful sigh and laid her cheek upon his chest again. "I know. The thieves' raid."

"Nay, I've another task to complete. I shan't return until this time on the morrow."

She slid over and snuggled at his side. Her bright blue gaze followed the swirl of her finger over one of his nipples. It made him suck in a breath and snatch her hand up.

"Are you listening to me?"

She nodded, her eyes finally rising to snare him with a glittering look. "How can I not? You speak of abandoning me here with your men, all of which are but strangers to me. And then there's your lover, Grizella…"

"'Tis only for a day's time. And she is no longer my lover."

Salena snorted and turned her bare back to him. She reached down and dragged the extra bearskin up and covered herself with it. "That is not what I see in her eyes."

Her voice came out muffled against the rock wall. He heard the tone of jealousy and it gave him hope. His first instinct was to tap into her thoughts, but no. He loved this woman. He longed to one day hear her profess her love for him. Therefore, he would give Salene her own thoughts. Somehow, that monumental event seemed much more appealing coming from her mouth voluntarily rather than by unfair thought invasion.

"She has been ordered to stay clear of you. You do the same with her. Besides, she is aware the relationship we had was not serious. She will get over it and you will both be friends before you know it. It is Grizella's way to be protective of all of my men when a new person joins our ranks."

"Is that what I've done?" She turned only her head and shot him a smoldering look over that elegant shoulder. Her tone reached an unmistakable high note that indicated coming ire. "Joined your ranks?"

He sighed. "That you have."

"I need to go home or at least send a note that I am alive and well. My brother worries over my safety."

"Your brother prays for your death."

"My *brother* prays for my death?" she gasped, clapping a hand over her mouth. "How dare you say such a thing of Sheldon? He would never think of doing such a thing."

"Loving? I do not think so."

"Oh, so you speak of this death plot again. And it is now your firm opinion that my own brother plans my permanent demise?"

Falcon sighed with a warning tone. "Salena, there is no sense in us going into that again. It is obvious you will never believe it. Unless…"

"Unless?"

Unless I get hold of that letter.

"Never mind. What matters is that you will stay here with me for as long as I wish it. Even if I did not know your heart accepts it, I would still demand it of you."

"I do not want to stay here and be used as a plaything by you and your men—or to deal with Grizella's spiteful jealousies. I need to go home. This…this cannot continue."

Home? Never. To her he said, "You are not a plaything. You've given both John and I an honorable gift. You will always be held in the highest respect by both the two of us, and by my clan. And if you do not wish, you will not ever have to make love that way again—except with me."

"Oh, well, thank you very much. I feel so much cleaner now."

"Salena, you enjoyed it immensely. Do not play coy or indignant with me when I know better. Admit what is in your heart."

She sat up and slapped her thigh. "Oh, all right. I admit it. I am a harlot. *Your* harlot, *John's* harlot. Whoever the bloody hell wants me can have me!"

Visions of what she spat at him seemed to slap him in the face. He shot up onto one elbow. "*No* one but me—and John if you so wish—will *ever* have you, do you hear me?"

Tears of relief sparkled in her eyes. "Do you promise me?"

His lungs ached in his chest. He tucked a lock of hair behind her ear. "Oh, aye, you have my word on it, forever and eternity."

She let out a long breath. "And truly, if I choose not to allow John to join us again, you will not be disappointed in me or seek another?"

"I promise you I will not seek another."

She drew up her legs and wrapped her arms around them. With her chin planted on her knees, she whispered, "B-but what if you both need…need the energy or whatever. I thought you were to make love together with one woman to achieve it."

He chuckled and cupped her jaw, rubbing his thumb over her cheek. "We gain soul-reviving energy with a single mate as well. It is just not nearly as long-lasting and strong as when we couple together with one woman."

Her lips curved ever-so slightly at the corners. "So one of you must mate *many* times with a single woman to attain the same effect as you get together with one woman?"

He nodded. "And I do not think I'll be lacking in energy where you and I are concerned."

"But what of John? Will he seek a mate like…like—"

"Like my insatiable Ice Princess?"

She grinned wickedly and he fell in love a small measure more. He continued to caress her face, marveling at the satin texture of her skin. "Aye, like your Ice Princess."

"John will find his way. He is not hard on the eyes, thus I'm sure he will have no trouble finding a wanton—" he winked, "—woman such as yourself to energize his soul."

She lowered her lids and spoke softly. "Well, if he does not, I suppose I could oblige on a minimum basis until he finds his woman. But please," she said huskily, her eyes moving back to his, "I only want you, my thief of desire. No one, not even John, captures my eye like you do. I will do it for you...and because I feel a friendly connection to John—as your soul-brother—and do not wish him to suffer."

"Salena..." His heart flipped in his chest. Her words had been as close to a profession of love as he could ever hope for. Falcon wrapped her in his arms and drew in her heady aroma. "Thank you, my love. And I'm sure John thanks you, as well."

He lowered her to the bed and tucked the bearskin around her. Crawling to the bundle he'd left near the door earlier, he snatched it up and brought it back to her. "Hungry?"

She nodded eagerly, her eyes lighting with an almost impish gleam. "Famished."

"Here." He tossed the leather pouch to her. "Some of the roast hog, a container of water and an apple. Eat."

She sat up and tore into the contents of the pack. Around bites, she asked, "Did you pilfer this from some poor farmer?"

He grinned, unable to resist her humor. "Nay, from your betrothed."

Salena gasped, laughing against her will. "You are incorrigible. He will hunt you down."

His grin faded. "If he has half his wits about him, the only thing he should come after me for is you." He clenched his jaw. "But he will never have you. Ever."

"You intend to keep me forever, do you?" She tipped her head back and took a long sip of water from the small flagon.

"Forever."

Her eyes scanned the cave. She took a crunchy bite from the apple. "And this will be our castle?"

"Nay, I have a small estate north of here. If you do not wish to go on these raids with me, you will be free to stay behind. In fact, I insist that you do. It will be safer."

Her chin rose in defiance. "I can defend myself — as long as it is not some outlaw casting an unfair spell of paralyzation upon me."

Falcon threw his head back and roared. Ah, but she was a delight to have around. "I do so look forward to having you in my company — forever."

Her mischievous smile faded. "You promise it will be only me forever?"

"I promise on my immortal heart." He made an X over his chest.

"Not Grizella?"

"Never Grizella, ever again."

She tied the bundle back up and tossed it aside. Patting the bed, she whispered, "Then come here, thief, and hold me. Rest with me until you must depart on your mysterious journey into the night."

He wanted to do nothing but what she asked. And he did, climbing beneath the fur with her. Her small naked body emitted warmth and energy. He closed his eyes, soaking in the aura of her. Yes, he loved her with all his heart, and it seemed with each passing moment, the emotion intensified tenfold.

Salina sighed and wiggled her ass against his soft cock, her back to him as they lay spoon-fashion within the bed gazing at the waning fire.

He combed his hand through her hair. "Sleep now. When you're off in slumber land, I will slip away and be on my way. Already, I cannot wait to see you again."

"And I you," she rasped, her body relaxing into his. "Falcon Montague…" Salena let out a long yawn. "If this is due to some…spell you've cast on me…please, do not reverse it."

"Eh," he murmured in her ear. "You are the one who has cast a spell upon *me*, love."

She didn't reply. He lay there for a long while listening to her even breathing. Sure that she had truly dropped off into a deep sleep, he finally rose and slipped from the cave.

The snow had stopped, leaving behind a six-inch white blanket that glowed a soft blue in the moonlight…like her eyes. His heart swelled. All he wished to do was race to Wyngate Hall and get his hands on that document as soon as possible. If only his abilities included that of disappearance and high speeds of travel like John's. He could be there and back within an hour, and right back in her arms with the proof he needed to keep her safe once and for all.

But it was not so. And he could not ask it of John. Accepting of the facts, Falcon sought out his friend.

"I depart now."

John lounged beneath a leather tarp strung between four wooden posts. He was stretched out on a bear's pelt thrown over the snow. The bonfire was close enough to afford him enough warmth to keep him dry and comfortable for the night until time to venture out on the excursion. He had his arms folded beneath his head and his ankles crossed. And he appeared to be a man much sated.

His ice-blue gaze flitted to Falcon. "Godspeed. Are you sure you do not wish me to travel with you or go in your stead?"

"Nay. I thank you, though. I'd prefer you stay and keep a close eye on her. She is not *tazired*, and I wish not to do so at this point. But I do not think she will attempt to leave. Things have much improved between us…"

"She is quite a lady. You are a lucky man." Over Falcon's shoulder, John stared up at the starless sky, his voice thoughtful, almost serene.

"I've come to discover I love her, if you can believe such a thing." Falcon chuckled, securing his longbow and arrows across his back.

John's calm gaze slid back to Falcon. "Aye, I can believe it. It shows in your eyes and in everything about you. Grizella is beside herself."

Falcon grinned. "Somehow, I trust you will be able to rectify that in no time."

"That I'm sure of. As you know, Griz is loyal, but she is vulnerable to sexual wiles — which I am not deficient in."

Falcon roared with laughter. "That I am aware. As now is Salena."

John sat up resting his brawny forearms on his up-drawn knees. "Yet I sense she does not wish to repeat the process."

"Nay," Falcon said softly. "She claims if you're in desperate need of re-energizing yourself, she will oblige, but does not desire it to be a way of life. Oh, she definitely enjoyed your talents, but she is apparently a one-man woman."

John nodded. "I can understand that. It is the normal wish of a woman in love to have only one man's touch."

"In love?"

"Aye, though she does not accept it yet, I believe her to be in love with you, brother. And I envy you to no end."

Falcon's heart swelled. He could easily invade her thoughts to confirm it, but no. He wished to wait and hope for those words to cross that sharp tongue and plump lips. If only it were true! Yes, Salena was definitely addicted to his lovemaking, but that did not equate with love. But someday, she would love him, and that he vowed to make his sole purpose — after this journey commenced.

"Your time will come, John. Lorcan, no doubt, knows all about it."

"Eh." He waved a hand. "Lorcan is nothing but a daft old wizard. His rants and babbling raves are a waste of time."

"One day, friend," Falcon said as he started to walk away, "you will learn otherwise."

"Have a safe journey, Montague. I shall look after your woman's welfare."

"Much thanks, Little John." Falcon waved and went in search of Warrior.

Distracted by his plans, he barely registered the sight of Grizella standing on the edge of camp in a deep conversation with Lathrop, the injured man brought back with them from Sheldon Tremayne's party.

Chapter Nine

Salena awoke with a start. Through the cave opening, she could see the black of the sky. The clouds had cleared and pinpoint stars scattered over its expanse like slivers of shattered crystal. She could see a copse of gnarled, leafless, snow-sprinkled trees against the full yellow moon. Inside the cave's space, the fire had long since died out. It was so cold that she could see her breath coming out in puffs against the moonlight. Though her body was nice and toasty warm beneath the pelt, her head was chilled to the skull. She burrowed deeper in the fur and tried to go back to sleep. The more she slept, she thought, the sooner it would seem that Falcon would return.

She had just slipped back into the blissful rim of sleep when she heard the voice.

"Milady?" came the gruff whisper.

She bolted upright dragging the fur with her. Clutching the bearskin to her naked breasts, she screeched, "Who's there? What do you want?"

"'Tis Lathrop, yer brother's footman."

He moved closer and her heart leapt into a frantic rhythm. "If you do not leave me this instant, I shall scream!"

"Do not be frightened, Lady Tremayne. I am here to help you escape back to Wyngate Hall." He moved into the lunar beams and she did, indeed, see that it was Lathrop. She'd never spoken but polite greetings to him in the past, so his voice did not sound familiar to her. But his mousy-brown, scraggly hair and thin body structure could not be mistaken.

His words sank in. Back home? She finally had an opportunity, unattended by Falcon, to escape? Did she want to?

"B-but…"

"Thanks to a sympathizer in the thief's band of men, I've a small wagon tethered to a mule a ways up the path," he murmured gruffly. "You can hide in the straw beneath the tarp until we get nearer the keep on the morrow."

I'm finally free to go. So why did she feel this utter sense of loss and sadness at the prospect? All she could do was stare at Lathrop's thin silhouette against the moonlight. Her teeth began to chatter yet perspiration pooled between her breasts.

"But the m-master of this—"

He snorted. "Aye, that ruthless Robin Hood. I saw him before he tore out of here hours ago, cavorting with that Grizella woman. Shameless bastard he be, and so soon after forcing himself upon you, milady."

"Cavorting?" Suddenly, she felt ill, completely nauseated.

"Oh, you can bet, cavorting. The damn scalawag dipped his cock between her legs, right after he came from your—" She heard him gulp. "Ah, pardon me for subjecting you to such nasty language. Forgive me, Lady Tremayne."

The bile rose and threatened to hurl onto the man. Falcon made love with that jealous she-cat? And right after leaving her bed and telling her she was his forever? Tears stung her eyes even as the anger simmered deep in her chest. She'd given wholly of herself. She'd even given *more* than any woman ever expected to give by offering herself to Falcon and John at the same time. And all so they could energize their immortal souls? *And because she—no! Don't say it, Salena. Don't even think it.* Never, ever again would she allow herself to be duped by any man.

The bastard!

"Lady Tremayne?"

"It's…it's all right, Lathrop. I'm just…thinking."

"Of course." She heard him shift as if he struggled to remain patient.

All the while, her heart ached, her pulse pounded with anger and she could not stop the silent tears. They poured over her cheeks in droplets of cold moisture. Grateful for the dim moonlight to hide her torrid emotions, she choked out, "You say there's a mule nearby with a cart?"

"Aye. We must leave posthaste, before those left behind alert that bunch of hooligans who went on that scavenger raid earlier in the night. That Little John fellow is still here—we mustn't go crossing that giant—but he sleeps at the moment. Now is the time, miss. We must leave now, else forego our chances indefinitely."

"I-I must…gather my things, get…dressed."

He nodded vigorously. "Of course. I'll be waiting outside the cave. But hurry, milady. We must hurry."

"I—yes, I will go as quickly as I can."

He slipped from the cave leaving her to stare in shocked loneliness.

"Falcon, how could you?" she whispered.

But she knew precisely how. He was a lying, cheating bastard of a wizard. He no doubt used his dark magic on all women in much the same way he had her. Poor, unsuspecting ladies who think they've got themselves a charming, attentive man only to find out they've been made to be a fool.

Never again, Salena Tremayne, never! She'd return home, throw herself upon Sheldon's mercy and pray he found her a match who would accept her soiled body and offer her a home for the remaining days of her dull life to come.

And she would make it her life's mission, she thought as she fumbled in the dark and found her garments, to forget that scheming scoundrel. That is, once she saw that he's hunted down and made to pay for breaking her gullible heart!

She righted her undergarments and pulled her gown over her head. Next, she donned her boots and laced them up.

"Milady…"

"I'm coming, I'm coming. I've just to find my cloak. Ah, here it is." She crawled from the cave and emerged eager to put miles between her and this lair of his. It made her skin shiver with gooseflesh just thinking of all the carnal things that had happened there. No, never again.

"This way." Lathrop led her through the snow toward a denser part of the woods. He held up his finger indicating that she was to remain silent as they passed by John's lean-to shelter. He appeared to be in a very deep sleep. She could hear the faint sounds of snores. A quick glance about told her everyone left behind in the camp seemed to have over-imbibed on too much spirits perhaps. Or mayhap they'd merely overextended their body's physical capabilities by living this harsh lifestyle?

Her heart did a little flutter when her thoughts turned back to what she'd experienced with John and Falcon. Even now, her pussy throbbed and warm juices leaked from her passage at the memories of it. But she forced the carnal, forbidden thoughts to the far recesses of her mind when she saw Grizella lying there in bed with him, her eyes peeping over John's thick chest. She was wide awake and those eyes gleamed in the stray light of the moon. Salena's heart lurched for she expected the woman to rise and sound an alarm. But instead, she watched Salena and Lathrop like a hawk as they passed by, as if she yearned for them to get out of her sight as soon as possible.

Of course! Salena concluded. The woman wanted Falcon and John to herself. And allowing Salena to escape was her solution to that problem of another woman intruding upon her territory.

So, it was all over. Falcon and John had used her like a common harlot and then tossed her aside at the first pretty face that happened upon them. The she-devil in man's clothing had won the short-lived war without even trying.

And what did that say for Salena's abilities to keep a man? Well, she no longer cared. Salena marched past the shelter and followed Lathrop through the woods. He led her to a hitched cart just as he'd promised.

"Get in," he ordered, flipping the leather tarp aside. She obeyed, climbing into the cart. After one wistful glance through the trees at the cave she'd shared with him, she lay down upon the thick pile of straw and closed her eyes.

Once again, the tears came. She heard Lathrop urge the mule into a trot. And to keep herself from leaping out of the cart and running back to his cozy bed, she turned her back and burrowed deep into the straw.

Sleep soon overtook her, but it was in no way restful.

* * * * *

Falcon disengaged the lock on the library's veranda door and slipped into the room. The library had a chill in the air as if it hadn't been used in days. The pungent odor of lingering cigar smoke previously soaked into the draperies assaulted his nose. Despite that detection, it was apparent no one was about in the manor at this time of the night. The entire Wyngate Hall seemed to be as still as a mausoleum.

By the yellow light of the moon that bathed the room, he could see his destination, the single side table positioned to the left of the hearth. Making his way around the large mahogany desk and scattered furnishings, he reached the table with haste. His eyes rose to the inlaid stones set above the mantel. Cold ash now filled the space within the hearth, another sign the room had been vacated for hours at minimum, perhaps since his last visit.

He eyed the stones and located the one he was sure had been removable. It was the precise location where he'd seen the man—a man he was now almost certain had been Sheldon Tremayne—remove the rocky protrusion and withdraw what Falcon had thought to be the key to the drawer in the table. And it was that particular drawer where the certain document was housed, the one the man that night had wadded up in anger, blaming Salena for what, he didn't know.

But he would soon find out...

He ran his palms over the cold, smooth stone. It jiggled only slightly, but would not pop free. A footstep abovestairs made him start, then pause. Perspiration dribbled down between his shoulder blades. With a set to his jaw, he swept the outer edges of the rock.

"Bull's-eye." His thumb found the indentation on the upper edge. He poked his finger into the hole and a latch clicked freeing the stone. Setting it aside, he narrowed his eyes taking in the moonlit little recess much like the cave he'd left her tucked safely inside.

He leaned in, his hand swiping the inner floor. And there it was. The key. He gripped it, pulling it from its hiding place. Sidestepping to the small table, he bent and inserted the key. As he turned it, a sound reverberated through the room, identical to that he'd heard while lurking behind the drapes that night. The drawer slid open with ease. Again, just as he thought, the crumpled document lay nestled in the wooden space. His hand snatched it up and he stuffed it into his codpiece. He closed the drawer, locked it, replaced the key and snapped the stone back into its cavern.

It was time to discover the truth.

Falcon spun on his booted heel and exited the way he'd come. He cupped his hands around his mouth and let out a soft whistle. Warrior bounded around the corner of the manor. As the beast trotted by, Falcon grasped his mane and catapulted himself up into a mount. He made his way through the quiet courtyard, around the deserted market and shops until he reached the drawbridge. Just as before, he *tazired* the guard and tore out across the lowered bridge. He heard the creak and groan behind him of the bridge rising back into place, but he didn't wait to see that it was secure. He dug his heels into the steed's flanks and raced toward the forest.

Falcon didn't stop until he reached a lone cottage in a clearing. He urged Warrior up to the lantern that hung outside the stable door.

"Who goes there?" An elderly man hobbled out from the stable's interior. He was dressed as a poor pauper would be in ragged clothes and a thin cloak and hat.

"'Tis only I, Otis."

"Ah, Robin Hood! How are ye, son?" Otis shuffled toward Falcon's right side.

He shot him a distracted look and drew out both a gold coin and the document. "Fine and dandy, thank you, sir. I've come to borrow your lighting. Here." He tossed the coin to the old man, watching as it tumbled, the lantern's light glinting off its shiny surface. "My payment for use of the lantern and for your silence. I've people possibly tracking me."

The man grinned toothlessly, both in delight at the treasure and at Falcon's words. "When do ye not have people in pursuit of ye?"

Falcon couldn't help but chuckle. "How is the wife?"

Otis' smile faded. "She isn't well. Has some sort of nasty, festering wound she got while out gathering firewood. I do not know what to do with her. There is no doctor who will come this far out, not without my weight in gold as payment. I was just out here in search of a horse's salve I could have sworn I had. But I cannot find it."

"I shall send Little John along."

"Little John? But why him?"

"Eh...he has a way with healing. Much like a doctor's touch."

"Really? Then she will be all right, Robin?"

Falcon couldn't help but reach down and ruffle the man's cap atop his head. "Sure she will be fine. You keep her well fed and comfortable until he arrives."

"Aye, I'll do just that."

"Now, please, if I may have some privacy by the light here?"

"Ye're welcome to come inside and read by the firelight, warm ye bones a bit."

"Nay, I am in a rush. But I do thank you. Now, go to your wife and care for her until John arrives."

"Thank ye, son, fer the coin and fer the hope ye've given me." He nodded and shuffled away, slipping inside the cottage.

Falcon opened the folded paper and straightened the creases, tilting it toward the light. He scanned the letter once, twice.

Yes, it was just as he thought. Sheldon's motivation for murder sat right in the palm of Falcon's hand. And he must go show Salena the proof so that she will not continue to pine for home.

He was just whirling Warrior back on the path when John suddenly materialized before him in a hazy mass.

"Falcon," he huffed, short of breath. "You must make haste. Salena has escaped with the captured prisoner, Lathrop."

His heart split in two. "Escaped?"

"Aye. It seems Grizella freed Lathrop and gave him means to travel by. Her stipulation was that he must take Salena with him and return her to her keep. I'm having trouble tracking them."

Falcon's teeth ground together making a dull scrape. His nostrils flared and white plumes of condensation puffed from them. "And why did you not stop them?"

"Grizella drugged me and the remainder of the fellows before I knew what she was about. 'Tis why I'm so hazy this very moment. I traveled as fast as I could in the condition she's left me in." His tone held an angry edge, and Falcon knew that meant Grizella would pay for her mistake.

"Forgive me, John, for speaking out so hastily."

"No, 'tis all right, brother. Do not dally with words. We must go."

"First, please go inside and see Otis. His wife needs healing. Apparently, she's very ill."

"Nay, I must go with you for Salena's sake."

"John, you can be inside and heal her, then still be well ahead of me in a flash as I make this journey."

John sighed. It was evident he worried over Salena's welfare. "Aye, you are right as usual." He didn't speak another word but strode straight to the cabin. He rapped on the rotting door and disappeared inside.

Falcon stuffed the note back into his codpiece and took out on Warrior as if the devil rode him every second of the way.

"Lorcan, if you can hear me, go to her. Go to her and tell her I love her before it's too late. And please don't let Sheldon get to her before I do, before I have a chance to show her the proof she needs of his deceit."

Chapter Ten

Salena dreamed of him. Falcon came to her laughing, mocking her. Behind him, John stood smiling smugly, his pale blue eyes gleaming like a tinted diamond, its edges sharp and dangerous. She rolled from side to side inhaling the acrid odor of straw. Cold permeated her skin in damp fingers of pain. She shivered, screaming when the two wicked bandits started to chase her. There was nothing else to do but get up and run. Her feet felt like blocks of numb ice. She trudged on and on, gasping for air, glancing behind herself frantically as she raced in slow motion through the forest. The rhythm of her heart beat in time with her footsteps and echoed in her head.

"Falcon, why have you deceived me this way?" she asked as she continued to run.

She heard the reverberation of his laugh behind her. He was coming, she knew, to cast another obedience spell on her, to force her against her will to do his bidding.

John was right on his heels. He came to demand soul-sustaining energy from her.

Why? Why couldn't he just get it from Grizella? she wondered in confusion.

She came around a bend in the forest trail. Snow was now piled up to the tops of the trees. Salena looked ahead and behind, and claustrophobia assailed her. An endless ravine of white flanked her path. There was no way out but to keep running through the deep gorge.

But suddenly, she could hear Sheldon's voice up ahead.

Finally, she would at least be in her brother's protective arms! He would save her from the thieves and make her warm and happy once again. Sheldon would be overjoyed to have her back and he would find her a match if the duke rejected his soiled bride-to-be.

The sky above turned into a cloak of black velvet with puffs of gray clouds. She let out a sharp sigh at the sudden warmth that permeated her backside.

"Ha, that is but a fantasy within the reality."

She gasped and whirled at the voice. Snow started to fall in fat flakes and through them, she saw an old man in a black monk's robe. His long beard lay stark against the dark fabric and it made her think of the snow around her. Thin and feeble, he stood there gripping a crystal staff in one gnarled hand. The tall rod glowed and she immediately thought of an enormous icicle set before a blazing fire.

"Who are you?"

"They call me Lorcan." He floated close to her and she shrank back, despite the welcoming warmth he brought with him.

"Lorcan? The wizard Falcon spoke of?"

"Aye, one and the same. Although," he clucked, "I'm sure he referred to me as *old* wizard."

"Hm, that he did, I believe."

"Figures. He may be the chosen one, but that still doesn't give him the right to insult an old man, don't you think?" He grinned all the while he made his point so she didn't take him seriously.

"Ah, yes, he spoke of being called the chosen one. But I wonder...why have you come to me in this nightmare? Are you, too, going to haunt me as Falcon and John are doing?"

He moved closer yet and that was when she saw the strange medallion. It enthralled her and made her long to reach out and touch it. The dazzling blue of it looked very familiar to her, yet she could not place it. It was on the very tip of her tongue but just would not come forth. She blinked when he spoke again, and his voice drew her eyes back to his. And she saw the eyes for the first time. White. All white except for the black pupil in the center. It made her tremble with a combination of fear and fascination.

"Falcon and John are not truly here."

"They're not? B-but I saw them. They chased me, mocking me in that mean way of theirs."

Lorcan threw his head back and roared. Winds swirled around her, stirring her cloak and gown. "This is your nightmare, Salena. You have made them that way only in your mind. It is not real. It is not the real Falcon and John. But you already know that in your heart."

"No, even during waking hours, they deceived me."

Lorcan waved a hand and a stone seat appeared. He sat, still gripping the staff, and gestured for her to sit beside him. Despite the trepidation she felt, she lowered her weary body onto the bench and sat with him.

Ah, but the bench warmed her to the very marrow of her bones! She exhaled silently before asking, "Why have you sought me out, wizard?"

"Because you are Falcon's intended, and you are about to make a big mistake."

"Intended?"

"Oh, aye," he grinned. "Not as in soul-mate or anything as easy as that." He tilted his head back and gazed at the parting clouds. "Oh, if only it were that simple."

"Sir, I feel no more less confused now than I did when those scamps were chasing me. Kindly explain yourself."

His eyes sliced down to her like two coal-dotted snowballs. Steam puffed from his mouth and nose. She caught the odd scent of him…ale mixed with ginger? Strange combination, she surmised.

"Look up with me." He slowly lifted his gaze back to the sky. She followed his lead. The ominous clouds moved off the canvas of the space above them leaving behind a scattering of winking stars.

"Yes, I see...the sky."

"Nay, look closer..."

She narrowed her eyes. Again, she saw nothing out of the ordinary night sky.

"Closer, I say."

"I am, I—" Then she saw it. It made her gasp. She cupped a hand over her gaping mouth. There within the masterpiece of space glittered a picture of herself in arrangement with the stars. It was as if she were a part of the universe!

"Mm-hmm." Lorcan clucked his tongue. "So you do see it?"

"Aye...I see it, myself in the sky. What...what does it mean?"

"If you could not see it, it would mean nothing."

"And if I do see it—which I do—what does *that* mean?"

"That my foresight is correct—which isn't always the case." He cleared his throat. "At least not in the way it looks to me."

Salena sighed and snapped her gaze back to him. "Why must you speak in such riddles? Can you not just tell me what it is you so smugly allude to?"

He rose and she watched his black-clad form start to glow. His body lifted upward and began to fade then glow again.

"Nay, Salena, I cannot. You must find the way for yourself. It is all already in your heart." He pressed his wrinkled hand to his chest while the other hand gripped the crystal staff. "Now that I'm certain you are who I suspected, I can no longer help in any way. 'Tis up to you, child."

Lorcan started to flicker.

"No, don't go yet!" Salena leapt to her feet and extended a hand into the hot air that sizzled between them.

He bent and loomed before her. The one hand let go of the rod but the staff did not fall. Lifting the medallion from his nape, he dragged it over his head. And he placed it over hers. It settled warm and heavy between her breasts. Tingly heat and a sense of power engulfed her. The familiar blue stone winked up at her when she tipped it.

What an amazing dream this is!

"I tell you, 'tis no dream. You will awaken with the medallion, the *Centaurus* I've been carrying with me through centuries. It is now in its rightful place."

"B-but I don't understand. No, don't...go." In one bright blink, he was gone.

She stood there watching as the clouds moved back in. Cold wind blew in, ruffling her garments and long hair around her. But she was so sleepy...

Salena accepted the drowsiness that overtook her. She laid down, curled up on the warm stone bench and slept dreamless. The mysterious medallion now nestled in her bosom as if it had finally come home to her. But the bliss did not last long.

"Wake up." Someone shook her, their fingers biting into her arms.

Her eyes fluttered open with reluctant dread. All she wanted was to stay asleep on the toasty stone forever.

"Salena, you bitch, I said wake up!"

The sting of a slap across her face drew a shriek from her. Her eyelids popped open and she would never forget the sight that met her eyes. That of her brother, Sheldon, his gaze blazing with hate as he raised his hand yet again and slapped her across the face.

* * * * *

The day had already dawned gray and cold with the scent of more snow in the air. Falcon rode as hard and as fast as Warrior's hooves could take him. He was only a short distance from Molly Pierce's inn when Lance came barreling around a bend in the forest path. His little feet trudged through the deep snow. He panted as he ran, pumping his little arms at his sides.

"Lance," Falcon said, reining Warrior to a stop. "What troubles you?"

His eyes bulged in what Falcon surmised was relief. He raced to Falcon's side and gripped his boot. Looking up at him with terror in his eyes, he gulped, "Your lady. You must hurry and save her!"

His heart skipped a beat. "My lady? You refer to Lady Salena?"

"Aye, aye! Miss Molly let it slip where Lord Tremayne could find her. They came upon the cart with the man Lathrop guiding it and your lady hiding asleep in the back. Lord Tremayne dragged her all the way here. She is in the barn strung up. Oh, master Falcon," he cried, "I've never seen so much blood!"

Falcon's stomach lurched while anger boiled his soul. He'd left her behind in John's care never thinking the man Lathrop would try and escape with her. He'd too quickly assumed Sheldon's rejected man had defected into his band. Then he remembered John's tale of what had occurred. And Falcon never thought in a million years that Grizella would betray him, using Lathrop, so that it resulted in the woman he loved being hurt or possibly killed. To drug his soul-brother to further her plot to have Falcon to herself, no doubt. His brows dipped. The woman would definitely be put out from the clan.

He inhaled deep and long and reached down, clutching Lance's arm. "Up you go. Quickly."

The boy was catapulted effortlessly onto the steed's back behind Falcon. "Hold tight," Falcon roared, and he dug his heels into Warrior's flanks. "Ya! Ya!"

The horse reared up and took off toward the barn behind the inn. Falcon came to a halting stop near the rear kitchen door and deposited Lance on the back portal step. "Go inside, lad. I shall repay you for this kindness at another time, I promise you."

Lance nodded and turned, slipping in through the back door.

Falcon leapt from the Friesian warhorse leaving it to root through the snow for stray grazing weeds. He crept toward the barn, his teeth clenching, his heart wrenching, at the thought of what he might find. There were a dozen or so horses scattered here and there, all saddled with evidence of being recently ridden.

He could hear the sickening sounds of lashing before he even reached the slightly ajar double door to the stable. Drawing his longbow, he notched an arrow and kicked open one rotting door. It creaked and slammed against a stall. Nearly a score of gazes snapped to him, his target, Sheldon Tremayne, standing in the center of the barn with a leather rein strap poised to whip Salena.

Falcon suppressed a wave of nausea along with the instinct to run to her. Her gown hung in shreds from her battered body. Fresh open lashes oozing blood crisscrossed the tender, alabaster flesh of her back. She sagged unconscious against thick ropes that chaffed her dainty wrists. Her long silky tresses streamed down her back sticking to the open wounds. He couldn't see her face, but he prayed it had been left intact.

I'll kill the bastard!

Rage such as he'd never felt in his entire existence simmered, threatening to spew forth. He closed one eye and aimed the tip of the arrow at Sheldon's heart. "Let her go, Tremayne. Now. Leave without incident or you die."

Sheldon slowly lowered the whip. His blazing red hair had darkened around his hairline and collar where sweat poured from his pale skin. His coal-dark eyes glittered with the devil's hatred.

"Get him!"

A clatter of activity sounded. His men sprang into action, raising and notching their own bows. Falcon reached for the door and swung it in toward him, the move giving the arrows' tips a sure target as they arced up into the high ceiling and rained down. The whiz-click of arrows in flight and imbedding in wood echoed through the room.

Falcon took advantage of the pause as the men reloaded. He peered around the half-open door and quickly assessed the situation. Since they'd stepped forward in a line protecting their master, he re-aimed his arrow and released it upon the nearest fool—he would get to Sheldon in due time. The iron tip penetrated the nearest man's lung. His bow fell to the dirt floor with a thud and he clutched the lethal wound, gasping for air. His breathing turned ragged as he dropped to his knees, blood now gurgling from his mouth.

He fell facedown upon the arrow pushing it further into his chest. Falcon wasted no time snatching a new arrow. Drawing back, he aimed again and picked off another man before the others could finish preparing for round two.

"Get him, you fools! What are you waiting for?"

Another series of arrows showered down. Falcon yanked the door in again until the sharp clatter calmed.

"Let her go, Tremayne," he yelled from the opposite side of the barn door as he re-notched. "Let her go and you will live."

The heinous laughter grated on Falcon's nerves. "You, of one man, seem to think you can outwit all of my loyal men, here? You are quite the imbecile if you think I'm stupid enough to follow your orders, Robin Hood."

"And you are quite the imbecile if you think I'm going to stand by and watch you kill her."

"Kill? Who said anything about killing her?" The mocking tone indicated just that. That he'd intended to kill her, which Falcon had long ago suspected.

"I heard you," he said calmly from the other side of the door. "I heard you plotting her murder, which is why I took her. To keep her from your murderous hands."

A long bout of stunned silence ensued.

"Heard me? Ah, you are not only an imbecile but you are obviously mad."

"Nay, Tremayne. I hid behind your study drapes the night she disappeared. I overheard you plotting with your man, the

173

very man, in fact, we took back to our camp with us after your lame attack. The man who now resides in my ranks." He deliberately said it to draw further truths from Sheldon.

"You wouldn't happen to be speaking of this man, would you, the one I just choked with my bare hands for disobedience?"

Falcon peeped around the edge of the door, his bow poised for attack. He heard a swooshing noise and watched as one of Sheldon's men dropped the thin man into the center of the barn. It did not surprise him to see Lathrop there lying upon the cold dirt floor dead as a door latch.

"Aye, that would be the one. And I thank you for that confession. We'll see that you're hanged for your...minor indiscretion."

Sheldon snorted. "We? Who would this 'we' be? Your Merry Men? Well, I don't think so. We'll see to their demise once we've got you and this slut sister of mine here out of the way."

"I have the letter, Sheldon."

Again, silence hovered heavy in the early morning air.

"Letter? I know of no letter of importance that you could possibly have in your thieving hands, Robin Hood."

"The one from your mother, the one that states the secret regarding you and your sister, Salena. The very letter that reveals some interesting details concerning who the true heir of Wyngate Hall and its fortune is. A very telling letter left behind by a dying woman, wouldn't you say? One that tells of a certain tragedy your mother endured—long ago and ever since—in regard to her son. A secret, Sheldon, that I will not repeat before these men but one that you already know well...as do I now, and as will Salena."

"No!"

"Yes. Your father always knew it, didn't he? Which makes one wonder just how Lord Tremayne really passed away..."

"What are you accusing me of?" Sheldon's voice rose in indignation, but it also rang with a note of fear. Fear at having been found out, perhaps?

"Oh, nothing, nothing at all. But it does make one wonder why Edward Devonshire—the very duke you originally set out for Salena to marry then began delaying—has red hair and dark eyes the very shade of yours. In fact, Sheldon, you are the spitting image of him."

Falcon pushed the door open a bit more, delighted to be afforded a look at Sheldon's face over the shoulders of his men. Already pale, his face now glowed pasty-white by the dim light in the barn.

Falcon went on, now having secured a captive audience. "Isn't that right, Sheldon? Even after reading your mother's letter with the sordid truth in it, you'd still planned to keep those facts to yourself. The solution, even more so now after reading the note, was to marry Salena off to the duke, keep the money in the family, so to speak—until you learned of the duke's gambling addiction and how deeply in debt he truly was. That's when you decided to plan Salena's death *before* the marriage so that you could inherit it all before she married and before her fat dowry went to waste on paying off someone else's debts. Or before it possibly became squandered away by the duke *furthering* that nasty gambling habit of his."

"You're mad, completely daft!"

"Nay, you planned her death. I heard you with my own ears that night plotting with poor, dead Lathrop there. Which is why I took her from her home. I had no choice but to save her from you. And now here you are beating her for 'disobedience'. What was the plan exactly, Sheldon, to hope you'd 'accidentally' hit her one too many times? What a great diversion, to inform the king she'd run away with a criminal voluntarily and needed punishment, but you'd accidentally punished her too harshly. She ends up dead and you end up with the entire inheritance. And the king is thinking all the while that you'd attempted to go after one of the most wanted men in infamy, and all in the name of His Royal Highness. Noble, downright noble of you, Tremayne."

"Look who speaks, I tell you all, but do not listen to his tales." He gave an exaggerated sniff and pushed his men aside. It gave Falcon a clear shot of his chest. But it put Salena, still strung up, just behind and to the right of Sheldon's shoulder. One little slipup and she would be the recipient of his deadly arrow. "Robin Hood. The infamous thief who steals from his king's very coffers."

He clamped his teeth together, weary of that accusation after hearing it for so many centuries. "I take from your kind— who first steal from their poor servants and tenants such as those you have protecting you today—and give back to them what is theirs. 'Tis the only fair thing to do when they have no one, not even a king or a master such as yourself, to depend on for a loaf of bread or a roof over their heads. You took their lands and yet work them to death, and then turn around and offer profits to the king to get on his favored side. But you didn't give the king all those profits, did you? And you told all these poor chaps that the king took the land and the money. You told them you had no choice but to take from them, when in reality, you lied, didn't you? All the while, you're grazing sheep on their stolen lands, raking in a tidy bundle each month and starving all these people and their women and children in the process."

Slowly, the line of bows lowered.

"What are you doing, fools? Aim! Kill him!"

Falcon continued to target Sheldon's chest. One by one, the men turned and lifted their bows, directing them at Sheldon.

His eyes bulged. Perspiration beaded on his forehead. "W-what are you doing, you idiots? Get him! Turn around and shoot him now!"

"Nay, we stand with Robin Hood."

Sheldon gasped, stumbling back. He brushed against Salena. She moaned, coming to full consciousness.

"Salena!" Falcon raced into the stable and pushed aside the men. Sheldon's panicked gaze darted around for an escape route.

"Capture him before he flees," Falcon roared, "and I will give you all an honorable place in my band of vigilantes, if you so wish." A pounding of footsteps on the dirt floor sounded along with shouts and pleas from Sheldon. They secured him, tying his arms and legs together with the remainder of the rope that had been used to place Salena in bondage.

"You thieving bastard! You—" His words were muffled by a rag stuffed in his mouth.

Falcon unsheathed the knife strapped to his thigh and sliced through the ropes that held Salena in place. She sagged into his arms wincing when her tender flesh grazed his hands. Her body felt cold, almost icy. Almost dead.

He carefully repositioned her, clutching her to his chest. Beyond the odor of blood, he caught her sweet scent. It made his heart still and his eyelids flutter shut. He kissed her bruised forehead, the tip of her pert, bloodied nose, her trembling, cracked lips.

"Falcon?" she rasped, tears filling her lovely cat eyes.

"Aye, my love, I'm here."

"H-he beat me. M-y own brother…he t-tried to kill me, j-just as you claimed."

"Shh, shh." He kissed the top of her head and nestled it under his chin, rocking her body with his own. "Everything's going to be all right now. You're safe with me. I'll never let this happen to you ever again."

God, I almost lost her! His gut churned while his pulse struggled to calm.

"'Tis my f-fault. I mistrusted you. I tried to leave when Lathrop told me…"

Holding the back of her head so as not to further injure her raw back, he leaned forward so that he could look down into her face. "Lathrop. What did he tell you? He knew nothing."

"H-he said," she whispered, the tears fattening in her eyes, "that you'd been with Grizella after leaving me. 'Tis why I agreed to leave with him, to go back home to my brother and my betrothed. Oh, Falcon! It broke my heart. You…you…did you?"

"Nay! Oh, Salena," he rasped, kissing her bruised lips with tender care. "Nay. How could I bed her — or anyone else — after having you? How could I when I'd already determined that…that I love you?"

Yes, he loved her, though he dreaded the day when she would die of old age and he would have to say goodbye yet again to someone he cared very deeply for. But how could he just walk away from her? He could not be so selfish and yet, he was already being selfish in staying with her. So why deny them both this time together?

She blinked, the tears rolling down over her temples and into the blood-encrusted hairline. "Pardon me, but did you just say…?"

He chuckled, kissing her again. To say the words had been like cleansing his soul. Only now he dreaded that she would not feel the same way. "Aye, I said I love you, Salena Tremayne, hellcat, spitfire, keeper of my heart, my very own wanton lady."

Salena hitched in a soft gasp. The breathtaking blue of her eyes glittered with a new round of tears. "Robin Hood loves me?"

He nodded and groaned, tucking her head back under his chin. "For the magic of Lorcan, aye, I love you until my dying day — which as you now know will never come to be."

"Falcon…" Her voice came out muffled, soft, almost alluring. "I love you, too."

He sighed, feeling the sting of tears in his own eyes. "Ah, Salena, I thought I'd never hear you say those words."

Starved for a good look at her, he drew her back, this time, far enough away so that he could get a glimpse of the soft swells of her body. And the sight of Lorcan's medallion around her neck made the universe halt almost as quickly as her words of love had.

"Where did you get this amulet?" He plucked it from between her breasts.

"Amulet?"

Her gaze fell to the heavy silver medallion nestled in the palm of his hand. Its heat warmed his hand, its mysterious blue stone entranced him.

"I…" She swallowed audibly. Her eyes rose slowly to meet with his. "I had a dream while sleeping in the cart. Lorcan. He came to me. He said that I am your intended. Falcon!" She gripped his arms and stiffened. "I saw myself."

"Saw yourself? Where?"

"In the sky, in the stars. He asked me if I could see it. It was as clear as you are to me now, so I told him I did see myself."

Her words were baffling him, yet he had his suspicions. She saw Lorcan in a dream. She saw herself in the sky. And she had the *Centaurus* medallion in her care, something that he'd never seen out of Lorcan's possession — ever.

"Then what, Salena? What happened next?"

"Lorcan placed the chain over my head and left me alone on the warm stone bench. That was when I awoke to Sheldon's anger."

His heart pounded, not wanting to hope beyond hope what this could all possibly mean.

With an urgency to get her alone and tend to her wounds, he said to the group guarding Sheldon, "Go and take him to the king. Tell King Henry the entire tale — with the exception that Robin Hood has sent you. Tell him how Salena Tremayne's own brother plotted her death, how you saw her whipped and beaten to within inches of her life by him. As a favorite at court, she will be avenged. I will send my man Lorcan along with you. He will see to it…that the king believes your every word and sends this man to prison. Once you have completed that task, meet me at Wyngate Hall and you shall all bear an honorable place in my army, and be rewarded handsomely for your loyalty. From there, you and your families can finally have decent food upon the table and repaired roofs over your heads. And I will see that you get your lands back that this man stole from you."

"Thank you, sir." They each nodded in humble succession.

"Much thanks to you, Robin Hood." The first knelt on one knee, then another and another. One by one, the entire entourage of Sheldon's former employees declared an oath of fealty to Robin Hood, Prince of Thieves.

"Rise and go do your duty so that your lives can begin to get back to normal."

They obeyed and Falcon stood, lifting Salena into his arms. He sauntered outside and inhaled the cool morning air, its scent mixed with that of his woman. The sun was just peeping through the clouds in a brilliant shade of orange. Birds fluttered about in search of seed. A squirrel horded an acorn and a rabbit shot off into the copse of woods beyond.

"Falcon!" Just before he reached the inn, he heard John's voice. Whirling around, he watched as he suddenly appeared out of thin air. "Grizella has stolen away with a small portion of our stash."

He shrugged. "Ah, why does that not surprise me?"

"Shall we go after her?"

"Nay, she will get her just rewards in the end. For now, I have other matters more important than a jealous wench. I have here what I need most. Grizella is now irrelevant."

John neared, his gaze taking in Salena's weak form. "What ails her?" His square jaw set at the sight of Salena's bloody, bruised body.

She moaned and rested her head on Falcon's shoulder. His pulse leapt and he felt a rush of protectiveness burst in his chest when her eyelids fluttered up at him.

"She's been beaten and whipped nearly to death by her own brother. She will need your healing touch, my friend."

John's gaze fell upon her with a deep affection. "I shall be honored to touch her."

Chapter Eleven
Wyngate Hall
One month later

Salena pulled the black mask over her head and settled it over her eyes. She saw that her sword and longbow were secured at her hip and back. Her cloak swirled around her body as she walked. It felt quite liberating, she thought as she moved to the desk in the study, to wear men's clothing. The freedom of movement, the warmth...the way the braies rubbed over her clit and kept her in a constant state of arousal. She simply dreaded returning home in the early morning hours and being forced to don those cumbersome layers of skirts and bodices once again.

But for now, excitement coursed through her veins. She must hurry, though. Her husband would be here soon to escort her to her mount. She'd awakened from her nap in a sudden state of curiosity. Her deceased mother's letter confiscated by Falcon in this very room had called to her. Until this moment, she'd refused to read it. But now, something told her it was time to address the puzzle of her brother and then lay it to rest forever.

All Falcon had relayed to her was that Sheldon had wanted her dead in order to inherit Wyngate Hall and all its land. She'd purposely asked Falcon not to elaborate. Just having gone through that horrible ordeal with Sheldon, and seeing the devil that had rode him, had been traumatic enough. Thanks to the serfs who'd turned against him—and to Lorcan's persuasive talents with the king—Sheldon had been sentenced to a score of years in King Henry's prison for his atrocities against her. At first, it had been difficult without him around. As children, they'd been the best of friends. But now in looking back, she recalled how he'd suddenly started acting like an ogre struggling to keep his temper in check. All of the sudden, he'd had her betrothed to the duke, then almost as quickly, he'd begun delaying the wedding day, making excuse after excuse.

The king, she knew, had as partial evidence, a copy of the letter she now drew from the unlocked side table near the hearth. Her hands shook as she studied the crumpled lines of the folded parchment.

"Salena..."

She turned with a shiver at the deep timbre of her husband's voice. Falcon already had his mask on, his longbow and sword in place in preparation for the weekly raid. Since their marriage, she'd insisted on participating in this noble cause of returning property and monies to the rightful, hardworking landowners. Her own people within and surrounding the keep had been reinstated with their lands and possessions. Those men of Sheldon's who had pledged their allegiance to Robin Hood had joined his band of vigilantes and excelled in their jobs, happy and prosperous for their families. Everyone began to flourish in one way or another. Crooked landlords were suppressed from their overbearing, selfish acts upon the serfs. Even King Henry was starting to curb his ways here and there, yet the Pilgrimage of Grace continued to rage on, flaring up here and there, giving them cause to continue in their own pilgrimage.

"Are you ready?"

"Aye, but first I must..." As he came up behind her, she held the note against her breast where the medallion rested.

He wrapped his arms around her and pulled her against his chest. Warmth and love enveloped her. She could detect that woodsy scent that told her he'd already been outdoors preparing for the foray to come.

"What do you have there, love?"

"'Tis...the letter."

He kissed her earlobe, drawing it in between his teeth, making her thoughts go to mush. "Your mother's letter? You're going to finally read it?"

"I feel I must. I awoke with a burning sense of curiosity for the first time in the last month."

"Ah, I can certainly understand that. But are you sure you want to read it now, right before we go?"

"Aye, I do. I must."

He removed his sword and longbow and led her to a richly upholstered loveseat near the fire. Sitting, he drew her down on his lap. "Read. I shall be right here with you."

Her heart ached at the tender support he gave her. "Thank you, Falcon. Thank you for everything. For rescuing me from my brother's plot to...to murder me." She shuddered, surprised it was still difficult to say that ominous word. Salena twisted on his lap and pressed a hand to his stubbled jaw. Looking through the slits of his mask that never failed to excite her, she added, "And for loving me."

"Nay, thank you for loving such a scamp of a thief." He leaned in and kissed her, his mouth wet and soft against hers. Fire swirled in her womb, but she held it at bay for the time being.

"Aye, a thief you are, of my heart and my desire. I cannot live without you, brigand."

He removed her longbow and sword, then unfastened her cloak and tossed it upon a nearby chair. His hand slid up her braies and found her vee. "Ah, I love it when you wear men's clothes. It makes the fight to get in there so much more tempting. To see you outlined like this..."

She sucked in a breath when he traced her labia with his fingers. But her hand shot down and gripped his wrist. "Please. I want you, there is no doubt about that. But let me read the letter first."

Falcon sighed and hugged her closer. "As you wish, milady."

Her hands trembled as she unfolded the note. And she read it silently, recognizing the familiar scroll of her mother's handwriting as the firelight danced across the fancy loops and tidy lines.

My dearest Sheldon and Salena,

I do not know where to begin, but I suppose with the truth would be best. I've instructed my loyal maid to present this letter to Sheldon upon my death, which shan't be much longer… In light of your father's recent passing and my current terminal illness, I find it necessary to write this letter to you both so that you may have concrete documentation.

Sheldon, though your intentions are noble and just where your sister is concerned, Salena cannot marry the Duke of Oxford. You see…he is your real father, Sheldon. Months after Salena was born, he raped me at a ball we'd attended. Of course, there is no definitive proof, but I know it in my heart, as did Salena's father. You are the spitting image of the duke with your bright red hair and dark eyes, while Salena's looks favor her own father without a doubt.

Sheldon, darling, I pray that you will forgive your father and I. To the rest of the world, you and Salena will always have the same father. But please know I felt it necessary that you know of your true heritage. And know, too, that your father and I loved you just as much as we loved Salena. The rape was unfortunate and a very difficult secret for us to keep, but we loved you no less for it and we often thought how lonely this house would have been if it never would have happened, if you had never been conceived.

Salena, sweetheart, I hope you will find a man you can love for eternity and who will love you in return. It just cannot be Edward Devonshire, though I suspect that would not have been a love match anyway.

God be with you both. And always remember your father and I loved you equally so.

All my love,

Mother

The tears trickled down her cheeks. "So that is why Sheldon betrothed me to him immediately following mother's death. He wanted to keep the money in the family."

"True, but once he learned of Devonshire's gambling debts, he began delaying your wedding date—which I am very grateful for." He nuzzled at her ear making shivers of gooseflesh spread over her body.

"My mother, she must have endured such pain and turmoil from start to end."

"Aye, I cannot even fathom it." He rubbed a hand up her leg stopping at mid-thigh, as if he sensed it was not the time. "Salena, we do not have to go tonight. If this news is too much for you...eh, let's just stay home."

She smiled warmly, dashing the tears away. Her heart swelled with love. Raising the medallion, she studied its intricate swirls surrounding the stone. "I'd like that. But do not worry. I have long suspected Sheldon was...different. It comes as no surprise that he is only my half-brother."

"So you're feeling all right inside?" he asked with a worried note. "I mean, you're crying and all."

"Oh, it is a bit bizarre to actually see it on paper, but Sheldon is already in prison. I have already accepted it. It is just sort of touching to read my mother's thoughts. It is...a relief, all of it. To finally understand and get so many questions answered."

He combed a hand through her unbound hair. It made her long to curl up and snuggle at his side. "Are you sure? Sure you're all right here with me?"

"Oh, yes! I'm fine and I'm not going anywhere." She dashed the last tear away and gave him her brightest smile. "You're not getting away from me, that easily, Montague. And I'll have you know, you *will* make love to me this night.

She paused and lifted the amulet from her breast, studying the breathtaking jewel. "I am so grateful…because of this, we have an eternity to make love."

He reached up and traced the pulsing stone with his finger. "Oh, aye. Keep the amulet around your neck and do not ever remove it. That way," he grinned roguishly, "I get to seduce you until the ends of eternity."

Salena leaned into him with a sigh. "I still cannot get over how lucky I was to be one of few woman in many centuries of existence who happened to be born at the exact time that the sun and moon were aligned perfectly with your personal *Centaurus* star formation. It was so awe-inspiring when I saw myself there in the sky of my dream." She pulled a face, a slight feeling of guilt settling in her belly. "Which would never have occurred if I would have been born the second child instead of the first."

He nodded, dragging his tongue down her neck. She gasped, bowing her head back.

"'Twas fate, beautiful, but I suppose I do have Sheldon to thank for that, in a sense."

She slid her arms around him, desire coiling tight in her loins when he found her pussy with one probing hand. "Please, let's not talk of that, of the unfortunate event with Sheldon and how he came to be. Let's talk of the amulet and how it will allow me to provide you with immortal energy forever."

"Ah, I agree. And always remind me of how much I owe you for that energizing power you give me with your love. Now, let's discuss those gorgeous eyes of yours…" He planted a butterfly kiss upon each eyelid making her heart hitch at the tender gesture. "There couldn't have been a more exact match to the *Centaurus* — thank the stars for that stroke of luck."

Her hand wiggled down between their bodies and found his erection. It poked out above his braies a layer beneath where his codpiece had been positioned. Just feeling the warm, moist tip with her hand was almost enough to take her to the edge of bliss.

"Oh, I did notice its color. 'Twas why, I believe, it seemed familiar to me at first sight. Now…" She kissed his neck tasting the beginnings of perspiration brought on by sexual arousal. "You just said you'd like me to remind you of how much you owe me for my gift that energizes your immortality each time we make love…"

"Lorcan, help me, the wench bargains with an immortal who can, at this very moment, read her mind."

Salena gasped and leaned away from him, capturing his wily gaze with her own. "Oh, I forgot about that, you cunning, devious thief of minds."

He chuckled, his hand moving to unfasten her braies. "I do not always invade your thoughts, love, but this time, I could not resist."

"And what," she asked, planting a fist on one hip, "did you read exactly?"

She watched as his breaths came quicker. It made her own do the same. The warmth and strength of his thighs beneath her bottom made her passage fill with a slow rush of cream. His eyes glazed over with that wild, untamable passion she so loved.

"You thought that you'd like to kiss my…rod while being pummeled from behind — for John's sake and my own, of course. The energizing, you know."

Her pussy throbbed at his confirming words. Excitement danced in her belly, remembering he'd once vowed that all she ever had to do was say the word and it would be all right to invite John in with them. Theirs was a different sort of reason, a customary way to these immortals. It was very common among those of their kind, she was learning, and just as accepted as monogamy was with mortals in good social standing. And all without risking the love of the initial relationship.

She enjoyed the thrill of it, as well as the giving of energy for immortality's sake, while never having to risk her relationship with her husband.

"It would be my way of thanking him for healing me after Sheldon's abuse of me. Oh, Falcon, I love you and only you. But I do feel this need to show my gratitude by giving him a store of energy as my thanks."

"Yes, at the time, I was not completely sure of what the medallion meant for you. But once I learned of its meaning, I was, nonetheless, still grateful to him that he'd hastened your healing, despite the medallion's ability to eventually do so. You know, it saps his energy to accelerate healing, and he'd already performed his mending talents on another wounded woman that very night. So, aye, I invite him in, as well, for a token of our appreciation."

"And you will see that Lorcan waves his hands and tosses some magic dust or whatever, to dispel John's seed from me?"

His eyes twinkled with undying love. "So that only my seed can impregnate you in the future?"

"Aye," she whispered.

"Consider it done."

She leapt to her feet, the crotch of her braies sticking to her wet pussy. "Then let's go seek him out. Where is he?"

"I am here."

Salena swiveled her head around, noting that Falcon did not, as if he'd been expecting John.

"John." Her voice came out throaty. She welcomed the pounding of her heartbeat at every pulse point in her body. "How did you know to come?"

"Uh...I'd already invited him along when I went to seek you out," Falcon admitted sheepishly. "He's been waiting out in the corridor. He...he'd just informed me his powers are dwindling. He needs a fix very badly. He had hoped—we'd hoped—that you might oblige him. But then you were reading the letter and...I'm sorry, Salena."

"No, please, 'tis all right. John, come in to the study and shut the door. And lock it. I...I'm eager for this joining as much as you are in need of it."

John sauntered over to where she stood beside Falcon who remained sitting upon the loveseat looking lazily up at her. She inhaled John's smoky scent tilting her head just enough to mix some of Falcon's masculine aroma with it. The spot between her legs pounded with insistent need, as if it instinctually knew on its own what would come.

John reached for her, enveloping her in his thick arms. "Thank you, Salena. I need this badly. Just today, I tried to *invisilate* from here to the hot spring for a bath. I could not get there. I had to go the whole distance on horse. And healing…'tis no use. I cannot mend a flea with the meager powers that are left in me."

She did not have to ask why he did not just go and find some harlot's house and go on a marathon night of sex. John was a noble man with other causes that came first. One just would not see him in a brothel or frequenting the town pub for a few swishing skirts. He sought out the energy when he needed it desperately and only then. John did not cheapen the act; he held the consummation in high, respectful regard.

And she was honored to oblige and to be chosen as this solemn, devoted man's mode of energy. It did, after all, afford him the ability to do good for others.

Besides, coupling with his soul-brother Falcon gave both immortal men far greater stores of power than single encounters did.

"'Tis no problem at all, John. I welcome your advances whenever you feel the need to invigorate yourself. Falcon and I have already discussed it." She leaned out of his embrace and looked up into his ruggedly handsome face. His icy-blue eyes had the power to nearly bring her to her knees with potent arousal. "I have accepted the ways of your kind and consider it an honor to…assist." To that, she couldn't help adding a grin.

"Don't delay," Falcon rasped, and she glanced down to see that he'd pushed down his braies and was already stroking his cock. "I long to feel your lips wrapped tight around my shaft, to watch John take you from behind, just like I heard in your thoughts."

She couldn't take her gaze from him. A surge of need barreled over her as she dropped to her knees in front of her magnetic husband. The Oriental rug beneath her knees cushioned her fall. She hurriedly slid her braies down her thighs to expose her ass for John's sake. Both men groaned in response. Warm heat from the fireplace soaked her buttocks and the moist lips between her legs. Salena bent and took the enormous shaft in her hand. Its rock-hard feel made her think of silk wrapped around granite. By the light of the fire, she could see the veins that engorged his tool. Her mouth watered so she obeyed its hint and stuck her tongue out, dragging the wet surface of it from the tight sac all the way up its length to the moist tip.

Falcon slammed his head back against the sofa and groaned. She heard the swish of John's movements and sensed that he now kneeled behind her. His large hands spanned her hips and massaged up and down her spine and buttocks. Salena shut her eyes on a moan at the sensual ripples it sent to her pussy, and she closed her mouth over Falcon's cock at the same time. He tasted salty and sweet all at once. The silky-hard flesh was unyielding against her tongue and yet it never felt softer to her than it did at this moment.

John's hand traced her spine from top to bottom. He cupped the globes of her ass sliding one hand down and between her legs. She drew in a breath around Falcon's shaft and tightened up in anticipation when John's fingers probed her slit.

"Salena," he rasped, raining kisses over her shoulders and back. "Your mons, it's so slick and tight—" he shoved two fingers inside her forcing a guttural cry from deep in her throat, "—with the sweetest fragrance."

"Ah, I'd have to agree with you there, John," Falcon growled, threading his fingers into her hair. "And her flavor...have you tasted her juices yet?"

Salena's heart raced. She knew they teased her. Except for tasting her honey on her mouth when John had kissed her in the cave, Falcon was very aware that the only part of her that John had ever tasted was her ass. What he was doing, Salena knew, was tempting John to do exactly that, taste her cream. So he did. He lay on his back and scooted up between her pussy and her braies, still bunched down around her knees. The feel of that tongue swiping her lips brought a rush of heavy heat to her vee. The flesh swelled and ached with want to be further explored. She raced her tongue around Falcon's cock, sucking and taking him deeper into her throat with each flicker of John's tongue over her clitoris.

But tensions were already running high. Falcon hissed when she tasted his pre-cum. John quickly changed positions and returned to his knees behind her.

"I cannot take it anymore. I have to feel my cock inside her," he said to Falcon.

"Do it. Take the power from her and give her back pleasure she'll never forget."

Their words of encouragement for one another ignited her libido into an inferno. She cupped Falcon's balls rolling the marble-like sac in her hand. With her other hand, she stroked him as her mouth went up and down on him.

"Hurry, John. I'm going to blow in her mouth if you don't hurry."

"Believe me, I'm almost as close as you…" And he found her cunt with the tip of his penis. Swirling it around to wet the tip with her dripping elixir, he gave her clit one more flicker before pushing into her pussy with brutal force.

"Oh!" Her mouth popped from Falcon's cock. He directed it back, returning her head to its rightful place. Hunger to devour and feast on him overtook her. She knew the same hunger gripped John. He pumped in and out of her, clutching her hips with an almost painful hold. Shimmers and sparks of bliss showered her body making her canal flood with sap. She tasted the bitter saltiness of pre-cum dribbles, starved for more. Salena reveled in the mixed scents of the two men who together, pleasured her beyond belief.

"Oh, yes, Salena," Falcon murmured. "Ah, you're going to make me come."

John's arms came around her, big and strong. To be the aggressor on one end of her body and the submissive receiver on the other was pure, irresistible heaven. But that did not compare to the expert twirling of John's finger over her clit at the exact moment she reached for the outer expanse of orgasm. It made her pound her rear harder into him while her fellatio dance increased to a frenzy.

As if it had all been timed perfectly, she tasted Falcon's shooting, hot cum at the same second John's warm seed spilled into her. The spasms of the orgasm overtook her making her jerk and scream around Falcon's cock. John groaned aloud, his teeth sinking into her shoulder adding one last pleasurable spark of pain to the mix. She swallowed every drop of Falcon's salty semen, her tongue taking several strokes from base to tip before she collapsed upon his lap.

"Wow." She panted, wincing with disappointment when John slipped from inside her. "That was incredible."

"You can say that again." Falcon wiped his brow and dragged her up so she lay across him, her braies still down around her knees.

"Thank you," John panted, turning to sit on the floor at Falcon's feet and lean against the sofa. "I already feel energized."

"You're more than welcome," Salena said with a satisfied grin. "But what is it, John, that you're so desperately needing power for?"

"Lorcan. He came to me, the crazy old man, and told me my time was up."

"Up?" Falcon's head lifted from the back of the sofa. His eyes were as round as two huge emeralds. "As in, he's spouting riddles at you about your fate and your future?"

"Aye, about my fate and my future," John groaned, covering his face with his hands as if he suddenly recalled something he didn't care to remember.

"Well? What's the damage, my friend?"

His hands dropped. He sighed heavily. Slow and deliberate, he turned his head and lifted that stunning blue gaze to Falcon. "His *Centaurus* which Salena now claims has been replaced."

"Replaced? By what?" Salena asked, her interest very piqued.

"By the *Scorpian*. Lorcan wears it even as we speak. He taunts me with the fact that it will one day be mine. And now that I'm aware—due to witnessing the *Centaurus'* plight—what that means, I fear for my immortal life. In defense for who knows what, I'm bound and determined to store as much power as this body can hold. To...to make my future last as long as possible without having to succumb to that old man's blasted foresight."

Falcon threw his head back and roared long and boisterously.

John frowned. "Why do you laugh so, brother?"

"Because it is obvious," Salena offered.

"Is it, now?"

"Aye, but first tell us," Falcon asked. "What color is the stone?"

John sighed. "Green. As green as the meadow on a crisp spring morn."

"Ah, well then, that narrows it down for you."

John rose, now in a bit of a snit. He clearly did not want to discuss this ambiguous future of his or be the laughing stock of this trio. Salena watched as his now softening cock got stuffed none too gently into his braies.

"Narrows what down, milady?" She only smiled wickedly when his tone came out dripping with sarcasm.

"Your search for your intended. You can eliminate every woman for the next few centuries with brown, hazel or blue eyes."

"Oh great. That makes me feel fantastic." He snatched up the remainder of his clothes. "The *last* thing I want is to be tied to *any* woman, no matter her eye, hair or skin color." And with that, he threw up his hands and disappeared from the room.

Except for the crackling fire, a long silence filled the room. Salena finally drawled, "Falcon?"

"Hmm?"

"Do you think he'll go and abduct her from her chambers?"

"No. Based on his aversion to settling down, I would wager it's going to be the other way around."

The End

Enjoy this excerpt from
Me Tarzan, You Jewel
© Copyright Titania Ladley, 2005

Jewel Dublin came awake with a start. Her heart went from calm and sleepily serene to sudden, pounding fear in a second's time. She hadn't moved a muscle, but her eyes now stared at the pink streaks of early morning sun on the ceiling. Slowing her breathing down, she drew in a long, audible gulp. Gradually, she turned her head toward the object that she'd instantly been aware of out of the corner of her eye.

Stiff and unmoving, she surveyed the purple blotch that perched upon the old highboy in her small convent room. Narrowing her eyes, she struggled to bring it into focus. Fumbling at the bedside table, she located her glasses and jammed them on. A wine bottle? Shards of fear pricked her gut. It hadn't been there when she'd gone to bed last night, and she'd not seen it before now. Which meant someone must have slipped into her room in the middle of the night as she slept. And for some unexplainable reason, felt it necessary to place the bottle on *her* dresser.

But who? One of the Sisters? The priest? A gift, perhaps, from one of the children's parents?

Her brow suddenly creased. But hadn't she locked her door last night?

Rise, Jewel Dublin. Rise from that bed and come here to the bottle.

The voice seemed to echo in her head. She sat upright and gasped, poking her glasses further up her nose. "Who…who's there?"

Come. You must open me.

Jewel clutched the scratchy, wool blanket to her chin and jerked her gaze to the left, the right, upward.

"God? Is that you?"

Oh, God, she didn't want it to be God! *Please* don't be God. She wasn't ready, not yet.

This is not God—at least not that *God.*

She flung the covers aside and scrambled from the bed. Her eyes snapped to the bottle. Hopefully, she'd be safe here with the bed in between her and the dresser. But if she found it necessary to escape, she'd have to pass by the highboy to get to the door. Which made her suddenly feel like a trapped rat.

"Who's there, and how did you know my thoughts?" She cringed at the panic in her own voice, along with the silliness of the question. A lengthy, deafening silence followed.

"Did you hear me? I want answers right now!"

A deep timbre of what she thought was an amused chuckle, rang out.

You will not be harmed. Come here, Jewel. Come here and open the bottle.

Emphasizing the man's words, the bottle flashed and glowed a warm gold, as if a yellow light bulb had lit up inside its purple glass walls. It pulsed in heartbeat rhythm. It beckoned to her sensual and hot, bringing to mind the buff men in the magazines she had hidden beneath her mattress.

"What...what's going on? I—I don't understand," she said, even as her feet seemed to step around the bed of their own accord.

Yes. That's it. Come here. Come closer.

As she neared, a tantalizing heat enveloped her. Temptation—that oh-so forbidden devil here in the convent--overwhelmed her. Her bare feet padded across the cold, raw, wood floor. Flashes of those nude centerfold men in magazines filled her mind. Hard abs, tight rears made just for squeezing, smoldering gazes that promised fulfillment. And...soft body parts that engorged in seconds and fit within a woman's passage like the rigid piece of a puzzle. Her panties flooded with excitement, but as always, she outwardly and expertly hid her desire from the outside world. Only she knew of the throbbing that plagued her sex. Only she knew of the painful longing in her heart to be held once again, to be brought to that pinnacle of insanity.

But never again would anyone hurt her the way *he* had all those years ago.

It's time, Jewel. It's time to experience a man again, just like those in your magazines, just like those you're fantasizing about right now, just like you once had so long ago.

She halted in mid-step, the bottle mere inches from her reach. A ragged intake of breath escaped her throat. "How…how did you know…?"

Open me. Open me, and you shall see…

The stopper, poised elegantly atop the bottle, glittered seductively; it charmed and enticed much like her centerfold men. Jewel inhaled and caught a whiff of citrus and wild tropical flowers. She tipped her head and furrowed her brow. Was that a parakeet she heard chirping? No. It couldn't be. There weren't parakeets here in the hillsides of Chastity, Vermont, even if it was late June.

She rubbed her eyes beneath the glasses and glanced over at the dull-gray curtains. They partially covered the open window and fluttered on the cool morning breeze. Streaks of tangerine and coral layered across the jagged horizon, blending with the lingering gray of night. Fingers of fog hovered across the pond down by the convent's wrought-iron gate. Dawn made a brilliant entrance…but was it real? Could she be dreaming?

No, it's not a dream, Jewel. It's an opportunity of a lifetime. Open me now!

Her gaze jerked back to the bottle. Well, she didn't believe a word of it. Her dreams were always vivid and alive with men and the world out there that she'd been hiding from. Just because it *seemed* real didn't mean it *was* real. But since it most probably was a dream, curiosity won out. It had been a stressful week teaching at the convent, so she deserved to indulge herself and see just where this dream would take her. And she certainly deserved an exciting diversion from the melancholy moods that had been plaguing her of late. These drab walls were beginning to close in on her. Thoughts of things and emotions long buried had begun to re-haunt her. Oh yes, she definitely needed a distraction. She was going to open the bottle and see what this was all about, what excitement might await her and help her forget.

Jewel lifted her hand and reached for it. Energy assaulted her, making her fingers twitch and her toes curl against the cold slats of the hardwood floor. She sucked in a breath and snatched her hand back.

It's okay. It won't hurt you.

Gathering a lungful of courage, she nodded her understanding. Stretching out her hand again, she gripped the narrow neck. Her body convulsed almost violently. The tempting borders of ecstasy reached for her. Heat wrapped with the luscious, just-out-of-reach edges of orgasm taunted her. She moaned and threw her head back. With a trembling grasp, she slowly drew the bottle toward her until she could cradle it against her chest. On a sigh, she closed her eyes and soaked in the warmth and passion of it. Her legs trembled beneath her long, cotton nightgown. The bottle pulsed in her hands and sent ripples of fire through her, hardening her nipples, oozing down into her womb.

And with impulsive speed, she clutched the jeweled stopper in her palm and yanked it from the bottle's neck.

Pop!

A humid breeze spun around her, plastering her high-necked gown to her body. Her short, loose hair blew back from her face, fluttering madly behind her. The morning Vermont chill fled her flesh and became replaced by soaking, blessed sunrays. She drew in a breath and salty sea-scents filled her lungs. Looking down, she wiggled her toes against the soft grains of warm, wet…sand?

"Hello."

The voice, no longer an echo, brought her head up with a snap. And there before her levitated the epitome of every centerfold model all wrapped up into one finely honed man. Sun-streaked, golden, long hair framed a handsome face with the most interesting aqua eyes she'd ever seen. He floated nearer and she caught the rugged, earthy scent of him. As he moved, so did his short garment, a strange rendition of a Greek god or a Roman gladiator. It revealed well-defined, powerful legs just made for...

"Jewel Dublin, it's time to change your life."

About the author:

Titania Ladley knew it was necessary to hang up her stethoscope forever and write fulltime when her characters started coming to work with her on the graveyard shift. A pretty scary prospect when a nurse is unable to tell the difference between patients, spirits and her over-active imagination. So for the benefit of mankind, Titania clocked out one morning after working a grueling twelve-hour night shift and dragged her persistent characters home with her. She marched in the door, tossed her bag of medical paraphernalia into the spare bedroom and put her trembling, tired hands to the keyboard. You bet she was scared out of her booty! But there was just no other way for Titania to live — nor was there for her patients.   ;)

Happily, Titania's never looked back. Residing in Minnesota with her very own hunky hero, one child remaining at home and twins in college, Titania devotes her spare time to family, reading erotic romances, walking, weightlifting, crocheting and baking fattening desserts. And arguing with her stubborn alpha males and kick-ass heroines.

Titania welcomes mail from readers. You can write to her c/o Ellora's Cave Publishing at 1056 Home Avenue, Akron OH 44310-3502.

Why an electronic book?

We live in the Information Age—an exciting time in the history of human civilization in which technology rules supreme and continues to progress in leaps and bounds every minute of every hour of every day. For a multitude of reasons, more and more avid literary fans are opting to purchase e-books instead of paperbacks. The question to those not yet initiated to the world of electronic reading is simply: *why?*

1. *Price.* An electronic title at Ellora's Cave Publishing and Cerridwen Press runs anywhere from 40-75% less than the cover price of the <u>exact same title</u> in paperback format. Why? Cold mathematics. It is less expensive to publish an e-book than it is to publish a paperback, so the savings are passed along to the consumer.

2. *Space.* Running out of room to house your paperback books? That is one worry you will never have with electronic novels. For a low one-time cost, you can purchase a handheld computer designed specifically for e-reading purposes. Many e-readers are larger than the average handheld, giving you plenty of screen room. Better yet, hundreds of titles can be stored within your new library—a single microchip. (Please note that Ellora's Cave and Cerridwen Press does not endorse any specific brands. You can check our website at www.ellorascave.com or

www.cerridwenpress.com for customer recommendations we make available to new consumers.)

3. *Mobility.* Because your new library now consists of only a microchip, your entire cache of books can be taken with you wherever you go.

4. *Personal preferences are accounted for.* Are the words you are currently reading too small? Too large? Too...**ANNOYING**? Paperback books cannot be modified according to personal preferences, but e-books can.

5. *Instant gratification.* Is it the middle of the night and all the bookstores are closed? Are you tired of waiting days—sometimes weeks—for online and offline bookstores to ship the novels you bought? Ellora's Cave Publishing sells instantaneous downloads 24 hours a day, 7 days a week, 365 days a year. Our e-book delivery system is 100% automated, meaning your order is filled as soon as you pay for it.

Those are a few of the top reasons why electronic novels are displacing paperbacks for many an avid reader. As always, Ellora's Cave and Cerridwen Press welcomes your questions and comments. We invite you to email us at service@ellorascave.com, service@cerridwenpress.com or write to us directly at: 1056 Home Ave. Akron OH 44310-3502.

Need a more EXCITING Way to Plan your Day?

Ellora's Cavemen

2006 Calendar

Coming This Fall

Discover for yourself why readers can't get enough of the multiple award-winning publisher Ellora's Cave. Whether you prefer e-books or paperbacks, be sure to visit EC on the web at www.ellorascave.com for an erotic reading experience that will leave you breathless.

www.ellorascave.com